FATHER'S DAY

Part III - Fulfillment

GARY KYRIAZI

outskirts press

Father's Day
Part III - Fulfillment

v4.0

This is a work of fiction. The events and characters described herein are imaginary and are not intended to refer to specific places or living persons. The opinions expressed in this manuscript are solely the opinions of the author and do not represent the opinions or thoughts of the publisher. The author has represented and warranted full ownership and/or legal right to publish all the materials in this book.

Outskirts Press, Inc.
http://www.outskirtspress.com

ISBN: 978-1-9772-5475-7

PRINTED IN THE UNITED STATES OF AMERICA

NORTH
TO EUREKA
REDDING
1
101
FORT BRAGG
101
CALIFORNIA
Pacific
Ocean
1
NORTHERN COAST RANGES
JENNER
101
LA SANGRE
SANTA ROSA
1
BODEGA
BAY
SAN RAFAEL
Pacific
Ocean
101
1
MUIR
WOODS
San
Francisco
Bay
GOLDEN GATE BRIDGE
SAN
FRANCISCO
1
101
TO SANTA CRUZ
TO SAN JOSE

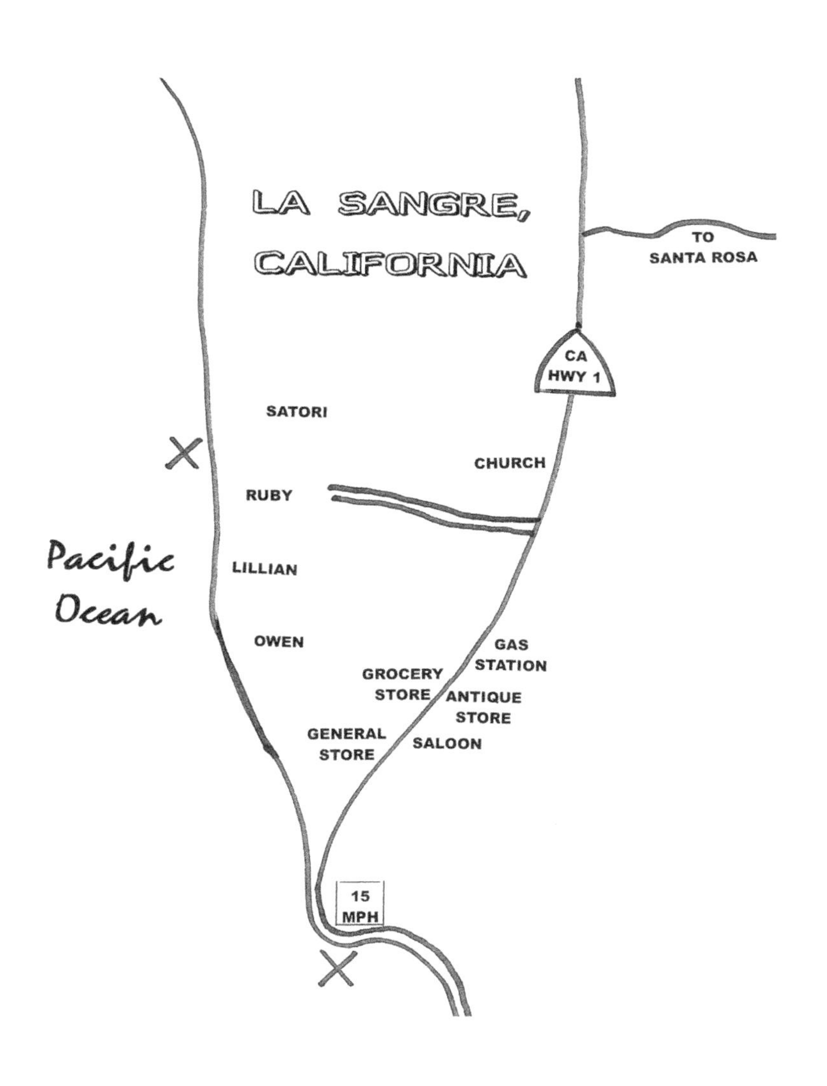
LA SANGRE,
CALIFORNIA
TO
SANTA ROSA
CA
HWY 1
SATORI
CHURCH
RUBY
Pacific
Ocean
LILLIAN
OWEN
GAS
STATION
GROCERY
STORE
ANTIQUE
STORE
GENERAL
STORE
SALOON
15
MPH

SUNDAY, JUNE 15, 1986
FATHER'S DAY

ONE

Constantine "Gus" Spagopolous and his 14-year-old son Demetrius set out from Bodega Bay, California, in their modest fishing boat, Christened "Helena," at 5:30 AM, 30 minutes ahead of sunrise and 30 minutes behind the high tide. As soon as the fog lifted it would be light enough and the high tide would be ebbing so they could anchor to fish a few miles north.

The daily routine was that they would catch enough salmon within an hour, then head further north to the dock in nearby Jenner, where Gus's brother Nicholas will meet them to unload the catch, and drive it to their small restaurant in downtown Santa Rosa, "Spago Brothers Greek Restaurant." Their boast of "Fish always direct from the ocean on ice, no refrigeration!" kept the Spagopolous Family business brisk. Today being Father's Day, reservations were full up for breakfast, lunch, and dinner. Gus and Nick's Mama and Papa were already busy, hand-stretching the phyllo and baking mountains of baklava, finikia, and spanakopita. Also, being the weekend, Demetrius wouldn't have to run off to school after the catch; he'd work all day in the restaurant, with his school books handy.

"Where will we anchor today Papa?" Demetrius asked him.

"I know when we get there, Deme," Gus answered at the wheel. "I tell you then, like always." Indeed, Gus Spagopolous had a gift of knowing where the fish were biting, like his own Papa in Greece. Gus didn't think his own son had that gift, but that was all right; his boy Demetrius was going to become a rich and successful doctor, here in America.

With the compass guiding them through the morning fog, heavier than usual, they carefully followed the coast north from Bodega Bay, the receding tide keeping them safe from the rocky cliffs just a quarter-mile to the east. 30 minutes out, at 6 AM, they suddenly, weirdly, exited the fog into a perfectly clear morning sunrise. There had been no gradual diminishing of the fog, no sudden lifting of it.

Gus turned around. A wall of fog was behind them, like a high glass dam holding back the fog, perpendicular to the coast.

"The einai auto?" Gus stuttered in Greek. "What is this?" he repeated. He had never seen anything like this, not in the Pacific nor in the

Mediterranean. He felt fear, and crossed himself.

"Papa!" Demetrius pointed north. Just a quarter mile ahead of them a second solid wall of fog stood, parallel to the one behind them.

"I see Deme! I know!"

"Papa!" Demetrius cried again, this time pointing to shore. The two fog walls ended on the shore, marking the northern and southern borders of....

"La Sangre, Papa!" Demetrius cried.

Constantine was certain the fog had parted, just like the Red Sea, as a clear invitation to La Sangre. But unlike the Red Sea's parting was an invitation to freedom, this was an invitation to hell. La Sangre's rocky shore and cliff could splinter the tiny Helena, and their souls. "Cross yourself Deme! Do not even say the name of that town!"

The sun was just up, bathing the buildings of La Sangre in silhouette; the dark and blank homes staring back at Constantine like evil dominions. The ocean and seagulls were quiet.

"Do not look at it Deme! Put those binoculars down and cross yourself! We leave here now!"

Deme crossed himself but didn't lower the binoculars. "But Papa look!" he pointed. "The cliff! Below!"

Gus lifted his own binoculars and gasped. No! It cannot be! Not again! "Aux pateras mia ston ourano!" Gus crossed himself again.

At the bottom of the cliff a body lay among the rocks.

Three times now. Three.

“Oh no!” Gus cried out. “I can not tell, Deme, is it a man or a woman? Is it plump or skinny. Your Aunt Theresa, my crazy sister, she lives there, with her skinny mechanic husband! She’s having her baby today!”

“I can’t tell Papa! I don’t know!”

“Aux Theos nha mhn einai iii Theresa! ” Gus cried out. God, let it not be Theresa.

“Amen!” Deme responded, still looking through the binoculars. “But Papa, I don’t think it’s Aunt Theresa.”

“I pray not. But we call the Costa Guard, now!” Gus went to their simple radio, good for calling for help if not much else.

“No Papa, not the Coast Guard. It’s 9-1-1 Emergency!”

Gus dialed 9-1-1. They answered immediately. “Hello, hello, Costa Guard? Yparchei ein ptoma stou brachia sto La Sangren, ein ptoma enos andhra....”

“Papa, let me,” Demetrius took the mic from him.

“Hello, hello, this is Demetrius Spagopolous. We are fishing outside of La Sangre, and there is a dead body....no, no, I’m not being funny, it’s true, there is a dead body at the bottom of the cliff in La Sangre! Yes, again!”

Three years in a row.

Gus and Demetrius crossed themselves again, and Gus said a brief prayer. "Aux theos nha lypithei ton La Sangren. Kai iii Theresa!"

God have mercy on La Sangre. And Theresa.

TWO

TRANSCRIPT
ABC SUNDAY MORNING NEWS WITH DAVE JEFFERSON
JUNE 15, 1986

DAVE JEFFERSON:
Good morning everyone and welcome to the Sunday Morning News. Today is June 15, 1986, it's 10 AM Eastern Standard Time. Today is Father's Day, but it has turned out to be yet another tragic one in La Sangre, California, where it is now 7 AM Pacific Time. Our Weekend Reporter Sandra Billings from our affiliate in Santa Rosa, California, has just arrived in La Sangre. We're doing a live hookup now...Sandra, are you there?

(3 SECOND DELAY)

SANDRA BILLINGS:
Dave...yes, we've got you now. We just arrived here, following a call from a fisherman who spotted a body lying at the bottom of the cliff here in La Sangre. Dave, the first thing we have to acknowledge is that this is now the third Father's Day in a row where one or more bodies were discovered here.

DAVE:
Sandra, do you have any information at all on what happened?

SANDRA:
Not yet Dave. The Sonoma County rescue team is here, two of them have repelled down the cliff to retrieve the body. The stretcher is being lowered by the rescue truck.

DAVE:
Has the body been identified?

SANDRA:
A couple of the townspeople are speculating on who the person is, but the police won't allow me to report that information until after the initial investigation. We don't know at this time whether or not the person is male or female, or if they're injured or dead. They're not allowing us to get close to the activity.

DAVE:
Of course. Sandra, as you said, this is the third year in a row something like this has happened in that town, all on Father's Day.

SANDRA:
That's right Dave. (Nervous exhale.) On Father's Day in 1984, football Legend Pete Freeman was killed by a vehicle on Highway One, whose driver then pointed her car to the cliff guardrail and ran into it, hurtling to her death. Last year, Father's Day 1985, Salvatore Satori, the Pastor of the La Sangre Christian Church, was thrown off the cliff, and then his attacker himself was defensively forced

over the cliff, by an automobile. So far this morning, we know of only one victim. Again we don't know the identity, or if it's a resident of La Sangre.

DAVE:
Sandra, if the past repeats itself, there may be more than one victim, is that right?

SANDRA:
Dave, you're right, and it's awful to say or even think it, but if this Father's Day follows the pattern of the last two, there would be at least one more. Let's hope not.

DAVE:
Let's hope not, Sandra. We'll be checking in with you again, after the break.

SANDRA;
Thank you Dave. Nathan Steer, author of the best selling *The Secret Of La Sangre*, is standing by, and he'll give us his take on what all of this may mean, whether there is a pattern.

DAVE:
Okay Sandra, we'll be right back with you.

(COMMERCIAL BREAK: AMERICAN AIRLINES, PURINA DOG CHOW, PEPTO-BISMOL) & STATION ID

Anne Owen rushed to the dirt road where the news truck was parked, in time to see Sandra Billings, the local news lady, talking to the camera. She had a scarf around her hair, probably because she didn't have time to do her hair. And her makeup was off; she probably put it on in the truck. Worse than that, Nathan Steer was standing by, being wired up by a sound man. How dare he? Anne walked up as far as she could get away with—she knew TV etiquette by now—to make herself visible to Miss Billings.

"Please back away," an assistant cameraman whispered in Anne's ear.

"Oh of course," Anne whispered back in a conspiratorial tone. "I just wanted to tell Sandra that I'm Anne Owen, Author of *Murder By The Sea: The True Story of La Sangre*. I was on the new Olive Gentry Show."

Clearly unimpressed, the assistant nodded and said "I'll tell Miss Billings."

Anne stepped back and watched as the sound man finished wiring Nathan up, then whispered some instructions. Anne fought the temptation to sneer and instead affected what she thought was an amiable countenance. But she knew she blew it.

The sirens had wakened her and Ralph, but it had taken her a while to get fixed up, knowing that the news media would be there and would want to talk to her. When she ran out to the scene she didn't see her husband Ralph around. So here she was, primped and ready for national TV, but no, Billings was already on and apparently wanted to interview Nathan due to his *hardback* book. All right, maybe Anne's paperback didn't hit the top of the *NY Times Best Seller* list, but it still sold a lot of copies and got her on the brand new *Olive Gentry Show*. Anne had never heard of Gentry and thought she was fat, obnoxious, and not too bright. Worse, Anne had to follow some plain-Jane who not only wrote a book *How To Marry The Man Of Your Choice,* but offered a money-back guarantee if the reader wasn't married within three years of purchasing it. Anne couldn't resist following that so-called author, whatever her name was, with "By the way, Olive, I'm *very* happily married to the man I love, a psychiatrist!"

Anne's appearance on Gentry's show led to *Sally Jessy Raphael* and most of the syndicated and local female-led daytime talk shows that were now the fad. All of the shows paid for Anne's first class travel, which she loved, and it kept her and Ralph apart rather often, which they both loved.

The director took Nathan by the arm and steered him to stand next to Sandra during the commercial break. "Sound check, say something Mr. Steer."

Nathan was a pro at this by now. "Hello Sandra, I'm glad to be here with you this morning...."

"Thank you Mr. Steer, you're good. Ready

Sandra? We're 60 seconds out."

"I'm ready Tommy," she nodded.

"And Mr. Steer," Tommy instructed, "we can't ask you to speculate on who may be down there, we're only going to have you discuss if you see a pattern here."

"Got it," Nathan nodded. As he and Sandra waited, Nathan looked over to where Anne stood, wearing her "I'm ready for my closeup!" smile. Anne Owen. The silly lady who had almost beaten Nathan to the book stores with her own ridiculous book about La Sangre. Of course, it was game-over the minute their respective books hit the shelves, as critics trashed Mrs. Owen's book as "a silly, tea party version of Steer's fascinating study."

But while an embarrassment (of which Anne was totally unaware), her tabloid-style book sold well enough to encourage several more self-proclaimed writers, all with shallow paperbacks on the subject, like the plethora of books about Elvis after The King died eight years earlier. All you had to do was deliver mail or gas to La Sangre to earn at least an editor's glance at a thin, poorly written manuscript that concentrated heavily on the writer's own personal life.

All of these phonies' attempts at a piece of the La Sangre Sandwich didn't just annoy Nathan, it really pissed him off. His credibility as an author was being qualified by those rip-offs. Now he had to wonder and worry about a book from Dr. Ralph Owen, the long-time psychiatrist resident of La Sangre, who must know things Nathan could only speculate. A book from Owen could bury Nathan's journalistic credibility; his book could be in danger of joining the *I Dated Elvis* books in the remainders bin.

But today was another every-dog-has-his-day moment for Nathan. He knew Sandra Billings wouldn't have interviewed Mrs. Anne Owen, even if she had showed up on time. Eat your heart out, you fat old lady.

"Okay Sandra, here we go," the director said. "Four, three, two..." He pointed at her.

"Hello again Dave. I'm here with Nathan Steer, author of the best selling book *The Secret Of La Sangre*. Mr. Steer is also been resident of La Sangre, for how long Mr. Steer?"

"Hi Sandy. Yes, my wife Julie and I moved here last year, just after the Sal Satori tragedy."

"Mr. Steer, I already briefly outlined the series of tragedies that La Sangre has suffered for the past two Father's Days in a row, and now it appears to be three. As an author and resident, can you tell our viewers what you think all of this means?"

"Well Sandy, as I said in *The Secret Of La Sangre*, this type of fear and paranoia is not unusual in small, religious communities, and...."

Over the last two Father's Days, La Sangre had claimed four lives: Corey's biological father Peter Freeman and crazy Jessie Malana died in '84, his adopted father Sal Satori and some crazy bodyguard of Jessie's older sister, Maria, in '85. Now, in '86, it appeared that even the chain link fence that the County erected along the cliff didn't prevent yet another body being claimed today, Father's Day, for the third time in a row.

Corey Freeman, formerly Corey Satori, was back on the wild roller coaster of his evidently cursed life. But rather than bolt, again, Corey swore that he would stay to help his mother, his baby brother Freeman, and try to salvage what was left of any sense of spirit and truth in La Sangre that Sal had tried, apparently in vain, to build.

So Corey fought the temptation to run and not look back, lest he turn into a pillar of shit.

Connie was sitting in her living room, one-year-old Freeman enjoying his crank-up swing. The phone rang for the sixth time this morning; Corey was outside with the other La Sangre residents. Connie didn't want to go out there, she didn't even want to know who was at the bottom of the cliff. Her husband died the same way, she didn't want to know any more.

"I'm sorry," she answered the phone in a firm voice, "we are not talking to the press. Please contact the police for any questions. Good-bye." She almost hung up when she heard a woman's voice. "Hello? Connie? It's Grace Freeman!"

"Grace? Yes! Oh I'm so glad it's you! The reporters keep calling."

"Are you all right, honey? Corey all right? The baby?"

"Yes, yes Grace, we're all okay, though the news people won't let us alone. They keep calling. The ABC News is already here."

"Oh, let the police handle them."

"Yes, that's what we're doing. They're not telling us whose body it is, and I don't want to know."

The two women were silent for a moment, in the bond of love and trust they'd built over the last two years, since the death of Grace Freeman's son, Peter, who was also Corey's biological father.

"I can't go through this again, Grace."

"Of course not Honey. Would you like me to come up there? I can be there in, what, six hours?"

"Oh Grace, would you? I'd come to you but I know they're going to want us all to stay here while they investigate."

"Investigate," Grace repeated softly. She'd had her own share of that when Peter died. How long is this going to go on ? Is Connie going to have to put up with this for the rest of her life?

Every single Father's Day? Another murder? Or another suicide? "And," Grace hesitated, "you don't know yet who it is below the cliff? Is everyone you know accounted for?"

"As far as Corey and I know. I haven't heard anything yet from the neighbors."

"Well I guess that's good. Anyway sweetie, I'm going to call my daughters and tell them that I'm driving up to stay with you. I know they'll worry about me being there, but they know I'm okay with you."

"Of course, thank you Grace. The police are making people drive straight through La Sangre. I'll have Corey give them your name and tell them I'm expecting you. They may ask for your ID."

"That's fine."

"Grace, I want to leave this town, as soon as I can."

"Honey you know you're all welcome down here, you, Corey, little Freeman, just like last year."

"Yes," Connie sighed, "except this time I'm not coming back. I'm not returning to La Sangre. Ever."

They hung up. Her phone conversation with Grace fortified Connie, so she picked up Freeman and went outside to the deck, where she made herself watch the rescue. Connie Satori was, after all, still some kind of leader for La Sangre, as Pastor Satori's widow. She couldn't hide in her house. But she also knew that as soon as she could, she was going back to Bakersfield.

THREE

Three days earlier, on the Thursday before Father's Day, Jay Carpenter was tired, hungry, and lonely. He had arrived in San Francisco that evening and found a hotel in the Tenderloin District whose lobby and halls reeked of Lysol over urine; but the desk clerk did accept Barnabas, Jay's Golden Retriever. The room he was given was dirty but the shower worked. After dinner at O'Mahony's Sports Bar and Grill, Jay returned and slept on top of the bedspread.

Jay certainly could have afforded something better, The St. Francis Hotel if he wanted to, but this place was convenient for the work he had to do. Friday morning he and Barnabas walked through nearby City Hall Plaza, and then east to Union Square. Further north in Chinatown he had a Wonton soup breakfast ("Zao shang hao, shen de er Zi!" the owners greeted him), while Barnabas had chicken in the rear. Then they walked due east to the Ferry Building, where Jay sat and enjoyed the clock's chimes, the ships' rich deep blasts, and Barnabas barked at the pesky pigeons. They then walked north along the piers to Fisherman's Wharf, where he got into a conversation with some fishermen, and offered to help unload their catch.

"Oh no Senor," the man who seemed to be in charge responded. "We cannot let you do that, longshoreman union rule, you know. Just talk, we listen. I like it when you talk about El Cuerpo y La Sangre del Cristo." He tossed a small fish to Barnabas, who caught it neatly.

"Gracias, pero venien Ustedes conmigo," Jay invited them all. "Te hare pescadores de hombres."

"Oh no Senor. When mi padre es muerto, buried, I will follow you, but for now we must fish."

After a couple hours around Fisherman's Wharf and nearby Ghirardelli Square, Jay and Barnabas walked into North Beach to Barbieri's Ristorante, where he chose a table near the open door so he could see people walking by and possibly ask them to join him for lunch.

"Ciao Figlio di Dio, fratello mio!" Signor Barbieri greeted Jay. "E anche Barney!"

"Ciao Vito," Jay stood up and received his Italian embrace. "Tuo business è buono, no?"

"Ah, molto buono, grazie Dio," Vito gave Barney a couple pats.

"Va bene se Barney rimane qui?" Jay pointed under the table.

"Si, Figlio di Dio. Va Bene!"

It was Jay's first full connection today. Everywhere else he'd start a conversation, maybe buy them breakfast while he drank coffee, but it never got very far. The Mexican fishermen were too busy unloading the biggest catch they ever got, although they did thank Jay for it.

After lunch Jay and Barney walked west on Geary to Ocean Beach, then south along the beach where Barney sparred with the seagulls in the shallow water. It was a long day's walk as they proceeded south, and by the time they got to Sloat Boulevard, Jay was ready for some nourishment. He went to the back door of the Doggie Diner across from the Zoo. The owner told him he'd like to have him come in the front, eat inside, but they can't take dogs. Jay understood so he and Barney had their hot dogs in the alley, chatting with the Doggie Diner help who came out for quick smokes.

Jay let Barney catch up on sleep in the hotel room while he spent the evening in the Castro District, hitting the bars, ordering a glass of red wine at each one. The various bartenders would have to do some searching below the bar to find a dusty gallon of Gallo Burgundy. Jay would sip, grimace, then set the glass down on the bar, put his hand over it, say a prayer, and then drink. Best wine in San Francisco.

He tried to make conversation with some of

the bar patrons, but they were evasive, with no eye contact. He finally gave up and walked back to the smelly hotel.

On Saturday morning Jay checked out of the hotel and he and Barney walked north, not stopping for breakfast, until they reached the Golden Gate Bridge. They crossed it on the east side walkway to the Vista Point on the northern end, where he'd met up with Peter Freeman exactly two years earlier. Jay sat on a bench facing The Bridge.

"Well Buddy," Jay reached out and patted Barnabas, who was looking at Jay with "Where now Buddy?" love. "Yeah, I know. We didn't get much done in The City. Now we have an even tougher job. We're going to La Sangre."

Barnabas looked worried and gave a whimper.

"Yeah Barney, I agree."

After 45 minutes of enjoying the view and watching the freighters pass under the Bridge, Jay and Barney walked over to the entrance ramp for U.S. 101 North. Before he could stick out his thumb, a car leaving the parking area stopped for him.

"Heading north?" the driver asked.

"Yeah," Jay said. "I've got the dog here..."

"That's fine. We can put him or her in the back seat."

"Him, Barnabas. Thanks." Jay opened the

rear passenger door, threw in his small backpack and told Barney to jump in. He opened the front passenger door and got in.

"Where exactly you going?" the driver asked him.

"Bodega Bay. If you can get me to Santa Rosa on the 101, I'll hitch a ride to the coast."

"I'll do you one better," the man said. "I'll take you straight to Bodega Bay. I could use some conversation. I think I know you. Next pay phone I'll stop and call the family in Ukiah and tell I'm going to be a little late."

"You can leave the restaurant on a Saturday night?"

The driver nodded. "I finally got a good manager, I can take more time off now." He held out his hand. "Jeff O'Mahony."

"Jay Carpenter." They shook.

"I *do* know you. But hey, how did you know I own a restaurant?"

Jay grinned. "I stopped in your Bar and Grill Thursday night, when I arrived in The City. Good meal."

"Oh yeah, of course. You were talking to Kristi, one of my waitresses."

"Nice girl," Jay said.

Jeff didn't respond. "So, what'd you have, at my grill I mean?"

"Jeff's Famous Beans, with your secret recipe."

Jeff beamed, not taking his eyes off the road. “Good huh?”

Jay nodded. “Very good, but I think I know your secret.”

Jeff lifted his chin in challenge. “Think so?”

“Sure. Bay leaves, oregano, and lots of garlic, but not enough to be obnoxious about it.”

Jeff turned to him. “You a cook?”

“You might say,,” Jay smiled. “Anyway, I especially like your giant wall poster of Peter Freeman.”

“Yeah, he was my friend, my hero even. I put that poster up after he saved the life of that kid in La Sangre, took the hit for him. That was pure Pete Freeman to do that, you know? He came into my place for breakfast pretty regularly. He liked my biscuits and gravy. The waitresses all loved him, he was friendly to them all, tipped them all real big. Signed autographs for the customers.”

There were a few seconds of respectful silence until Jay said, “I know. He told me. He gave me a ride north from here.”

“Oh yeah?” Jeff turned to Jay but didn’t ask for details of their meeting, only replied “I miss him.” He turned back to the road. After a moment he said “Looked like you and Kristi had quite a conversation. I didn’t want to interrupt because I saw her listening to you, so I had the other two girls to cover her tables. I uh...I guess it's none of my business, but I'm curious what you two were talking about. She and Pete were an item for a few seasons, you know; they were living together. It looked like an intense conversation you two had."

"Well we talked about Peter, of course," Jay said. "I told her he'd given me a ride up to La Sangre after he left the grill that Saturday morning."

"It was the last time we saw him. So...did Kristi tell you about the book she wrote and wants to get published, *Inside The Locker Room: My Life With Pete Freeman*."

"She asked me if I'd like to read it," Jay let out a breath. "I politely refused."

"Well I read her manuscript," Jeff creased his forehead. "I didn't like it."

"All I could tell Kristi was what I tell anyone: examine your motives for writing such a book. Examine your motives for anything, for that matter."

Jeff grunted. "She could probably make good money off something like that. Since Pete was killed, he's more famous than...." Jeff stopped and considered, "than Joe Montana!"

"Yeah," Jay chuckled. "I like Joe."

They were quiet for a few minutes as they exited the 101 onto Highway One.

"So, you're spending the night in Bodega Bay?" Jeff asked.

"Yeah, then I'll head up to La Sangre for Father's Day."

"Well, you be careful pal. I mean, if you gave Pete a ride that day, did you stay with him in La Sangre?"

"No, I left. I had a bad feeling about the place and told Pete so, but he chose to stay."

They drove into the green canopy of Muir Woods on their way to the Pacific Ocean.

Phil Stevens went out the back door of The Tides kitchen and emptied a bucket of fish heads into the dumpster. He was preparing the salmon fillets for the Saturday lunch crowd and always liked to stay ahead.

"Hey pal, you got one of those fish heads for Barney here?" Jay asked as he let himself through the back gate.

"Jay! Hey man!" Not much of a hugger, Phil reached out and shook Jay's hand enthusiastically. "How are you?"

"I'm good Phil, a little tired and hungry. Haven't had breakfast."

"Well, we'll take care of that, don't you worry. And I'll get old Barnabas some breakfast too." He leaned down and grabbed Barnabas' neck with both hands. "No fish heads for you, huh Barney? I'll make you a mess of scrambled eggs and bacon, how's that sound?"

"Woof!"

Jay used the employee rest room off the kitchen and went into the dining room.

"Jay!" one of the waitresses called from behind the counter. "Phil just told me you were here. There, I saved you the seat on the end." She walked over to Jay: in her fifties, tall tough lady, in good shape from clocking mileage throughout the restaurant that she and Phil were so proud of. Her hair was teased and bleached, pink uniform with a name plate that read "Hazel."

"Thanks Hazel." Jay gave her a kiss on the cheek, sat down and looked around. "Busy here this morning."

She placed a mug in front of him and poured The Tides' famous coffee. "I know. Tomorrow being Father's Day, tourists are coming in for the weekend. They're actually expecting something to happen there three times in a row, can you believe that? Just like whenever 'The Birds' is shown on TV, we do turnaway business for the next two, three days. Of course we can plan for *that*. We just double our supplies and increase the server schedule, with bonuses, and it means good money for all of us." She stopped and looked at Jay, who was mesmerized by her conversation.

"Oh what am I doing?" she asked playfully. "You know all this!"

"I love hearing it," Jay smiled at her. "So, is that fancy new motel of yours full up?" The modest-sized, one-story Tides Motel had just opened after being given fast-track approval by Bodega Bay, Sonoma County, and the California Coastal Commission, when the Bodega Bay Lodge could no longer handle the constant crowds. But they'd never be able to expand it, the CCC mandated. ("Just 20 rooms. That's all you get, ever.")

"Yes," Hazel said, "but we always keep one room open, for celebrities like you."

"Celebrity?" Jay raised his eyebrows. "I think John Lennon was right. I didn't do so well in San Francisco, whereas they had fans packed to the top of Candlestick Park."

"1966," Hazel smiled wistfully. "I was just a teenager. It broke my heart I couldn't see them. And now..." She looked out the window. The fog was still in. "I'm sad for San Francisco now. I was always so proud to be born there, I grew up in the Richmond District, just a few blocks from the beach. We could hear the laughing lady at the Playland Fun House until midnight, every night of the year. My sister and I would giggle along and fall asleep to her. Laughin' Sal was her name."

Hazel continued to look out the window. "Even as kids we knew that Laughin' Sal wasn't laughing at us, but with us. So we laughed with her." Hazel smiled and looked back at Jay. "And now, what I see happening there, whenever I visit..." She shook her head, sighed, and pulled out her pad. "Your usual? Three poached eggs, two minutes, grits, crispy bacon, sourdough toast?"

"You know me well."

Hazel smiled and ripped off the ticket and took it over to the carousel in the pass-through.

Jay swallowed the last piece of crispy bacon, finished off the buttered sourdough toast, and emptied his coffee mug. Yes. That was good.

He looked around. The restaurant was still full to capacity, and in the lobby and outside there were at least 50 people waiting and drinking The Tides coffee out of styrofoam cups.

"Fill that up again for you, Honey?" Hazel stood at the counter, coffee pot raised.

"No I'm good, thanks Doll." Jay wiped his mouth with his napkin. "I was just thinking, it's good to be home." He leaned back in the cushioned stool. "But I feel like I'll sleep for 16 hours. Didn't get much sleep in The City."

"I'll bet you didn't. You just sleep away, Honey, nobody's going to bother you. I already told Martha to ready your room. How long are you staying?"

"Just tonight, but I'd like to leave early, before sunrise. Do you think Phil could drive me up to La Sangre, say at 5:30?"

"Sure, he's here at five, same time as me. We

don't open 'til six. I can cover some of the prep while he gets you up there and back."

Jay lay down his napkin. "Well, I'll go ask him."

"Oh he'll do it all right. Otherwise there'll be no more rib-eye dinners for him. But Jay, just what are you going to be doing in La Sangre, on Father's Day no less?"

"Matthew 6:34."

"Wise guy. Go on over to the motel, I'm sure Martha's got the room ready for you."

He got into the bed gratefully. Clean room, clean sheets, nice pillow. It all had a sense of warmth and family.

He turned over on his back and ran his hand down his beard. It ended up being a great day after all. Walking across the Golden Gate Bridge, getting a ride from Jeff O'Mahony, and the warm welcome from his friends at The Tides.

But Hazel was right, he had a big job tomorrow in La Sangre. In the meantime sleep was what he needed, sixteen hours' worth, up at 5 AM.

Before drifting off, Jay did a millisecond review of the past year at La Sangre.

SUNDAY, JUNE 16, 1985
FATHER'S DAY

FOUR

PASTOR DEAD IN APPARENT HIRED KILLING GONE WRONG
by Nathan Steer
Santa Rosa Dispatch Staff Writer

LA SANGRE, California (AP) June 16, 1985. Salvatore Satori, 39, pastor of La Sangre Christian Church, and Bruno Logges, 32, of San Jose are dead, apparently the result of a hired killing gone wrong.

Logges allegedly hurled Satori over the cliff along State Route 1 just moments after Satori pushed Ralph Owen, MD, out of the way of Logges.

According to the Sonoma County Sheriff's report, Satori took the hit intended for Owen, a psychiatrist living in La Sangre. Logges was employed as a personal bodyguard to Maria Malana, 48, of San Jose. Malana turned herself in to authorities within an hour of the incident, confessing to having hired Logges to kill Owen.

Witnesses at the chaotic scene said that moments after throwing Satori over the cliff, with Malana screaming that he got the wrong man,

Logges ran after Owen. Owen escaped by entering a vehicle driven by Matthew Grant of La Sangre, and Logges jumped onto the vehicle's hood. As Grant accelerated and swerved toward the guard rail at the tight turn just south of town, Logges was thrown off the hood, over the cliff, and into the ocean.

Malana is in custody and state investigations are underway. In addition to determining motives, authorities are looking into possible connections to a strikingly similar tragedy in La Sangre during the Father's Day weekend in 1984 that took the life of two people, including retired NFL legend Peter Freeman.

In that incident, Freeman pushed Corey Satori, the pastor's son, out of the path of a speeding vehicle and was himself run over and pronounced dead at the scene. Jessie Malana, younger sister of Maria Malana, was the driver who ultimately hit a guard rail and was catapulted to her death at the bottom of a cliff. Both deaths were ruled accidental.

La Sangre is a small coastal town 85 miles north of San Francisco. The town's traditions include an annual Father's Day weekend celebration.

Nathan Steer had called the Associated Press from his and Julie's new home in La Sangre, as soon as Sheriff Daley gave Nathan—well ahead of anyone else—the facts. This would be his third piece for the Associated Press, with the two he'd gotten after last year's Father's Day tragedy: the initial report and then the State Attorney's ruling on the incident four weeks later.

Nathan's time was here. Julie had told him, repeatedly and patiently throughout their marriage, that Nathan's time would come, but his doubt prevailed. And now here it was, in print. Damn, if Julie wasn't at work at the hospital right now he'd make wild love to her. He knew—he *knew*—that this time it was him, his *talent,* not a fluke, not just being in the right place at the right time. No. Nathan Steer could finally, really, call himself a writer. A journalist. Now, if he could just get his book, *The Secret of La Sangre*, published, he'd be an author. First thing Monday morning, he'll call the San Francisco Writer's Agency again. Let's see them try again to reject his manuscript, which he'd begun updating last night after Sal Satori was pushed off the cliff.

Sal's body, and that of his killer Bruno Logges, were recovered from the rocks and taken away just before sunup on Father's Day morning, by which time deputies were stationed on Highway One at La Sangre, preventing people from pouring into the town. The crime chasers, who heard San Francisco's 24/7 radio news station broadcast Nathan's AP piece at 7 AM, jumped in their cars, grabbed coffee and a doughnut to go at the nearest Dunkin' Donuts, and drove to La Sangre. They were all sure they'd be the first to see something: the bodies, the murderer being taken away by the cops as he writhed in agony, spilled blood, grieving family members, something.

While most of the blood-sniffers were from Sonoma and Marin Counties, others drove south from Mendocino County and north from San Francisco. They hit bumper-to-bumper traffic within a one-mile radius of La Sangre, but they didn't mind. After all, that was part of the fun, following the rest of the vultures to leer at the locations and aftermath of any human tragedy: Dealey Plaza in Dallas where President John F. Kennedy was assassinated; the Lorraine Motel in Memphis where Dr. Martin Luther King was assassinated; Graceland in Memphis where Elvis died of, many wanted to believe, natural causes; the humble house on East 54th Street in South Los Angeles, where the Symbionese Liberation Army—who had kidnapped Publishing Tycoon William Randolph Hearst's granddaughter Patty—was finally taken out after a gunfight with the LAPD. All of this provided onlookers with a major rush, like waiting for an hour in line to ride a one-minute looping roller coaster, and apparently it was just as satisfying.

With Highway One a parking lot, it provided drivers an opportunity to turn off their engines, get out, and quickly bond with a stranger, that bond growing like a Sonoma County grass fire, fueled by wild suppositions about what may have happened and what had already happened.

Hey buddy, it's a definite pattern. I know, three times in a row. Yeah, all on Father's Day. What do you think about all those people saying that La Sangre is somehow inherently evil? Well my wife's into that. Hey Betty, tell this man what you said...oh, I'm sorry, this is Betty, I'm Harold. Hi Betty, Harold, I'm Craig. They shake hands and proceed with their titillating speculations.

"Crime scene, move along," the police waved the thrill seekers through town. "The gas station is closed." Northern Californians knew well to avoid the rip-off gas stations on Highway One. The La Sangre Last Chance Gas Station currently had its gas at $1.99 a gallon, a good 50 cents over the inland. Sal Satori, like the townspeople, always filled up his car and the church van in Santa Rosa, while keeping an eye on the prices there and maintaining the margin. All the gas stations on Highway One did that. It's just what they did, and their reasoning, probably valid, was that the oil companies charged them more to use separate, smaller trucks because the big rigs couldn't navigate the coastal roads. That assertion, true or not, was met with shrugging acceptance. Everyone was just happy that President Ronald Reagan had, so far, fulfilled his campaign promise to control gas prices.

"Crime scene, move along, the gas station is closed."

At Sunday's sunrise, Corey and Connie—with barely three hours sleep between them—were sitting on the deck, heavy coats on. Connie had baby Freeman bundled up close to her, her only sense of certainty. Salvatore Anthony Satori was dead. Her husband, Sal. What a beautiful man, that "Italian Stallion," who had to die before she realized just how wonderful he was. Yes, he was wonderful. Yes, he was human. When she—a pregnant unwed 17-year-old—met Sal, she thought because he was a Pastor (and a *very* handsome one) he was going to save her, protect her, and be the Perfect Husband and Father. She had told Sal on their first date that she was two months pregnant, and he just took charge and said "Let's get married." Connie liked that, the way he took charge. She wouldn't have to make decisions, not that she ever had before. Her parents handled all that stuff.

But did Sal love her? *Really* love her? Oh, probably, in the way that men do. Were her expectations unrealistic? Probably, in the way that women do. She was young, dumb, and vulnerable, expecting a lifelong 24/7 passionate relationship like the one hour of high school ecstasy that she'd had with Peter Freeman at the end of their senior year. Their resultant son, Corey, whom Peter knew nothing about, kept her passion alive throughout her marriage to Sal. She never told Sal, or Corey, who his father was. Sal didn't find out until both he and Peter discovered it in their first, and as it turned out, their last conversation.

Baby Freeman gave a happy cry, and Connie adjusted his blanket. Now, what kind of marriage would it have been if Sal knew that Corey was the son of NFL star Pete Freeman? Would Sal still have married her? Pete wasn't a star yet, he'd just started college. But years later, wouldn't a handsome football celebrity, wearing a Superbowl ring, be a tough act to follow? Wouldn't Pete Freeman's celebrity presence taunt Sal? She assumed, probably correctly, that it was easier for Sal to just toss off Corey's bio-father as, so she told him, "a one-time fling with a high school boy," whom she never named and claimed she barely knew. Sal didn't press her for details and she didn't volunteer any; it was a case of mutual evasion. That Corey's biological father remained nameless and faceless probably made it easier for Sal to pretend that Baby Corey was actually his.

But any resolution Sal and/or Connie made regarding Corey's hidden paternity was destroyed on the day Corey was born. When Sal saw that beautiful baby, all eight pounds of him, a shock of blonde hair, he was reminded that Corey was not his son, and probably never would be. Was this all her fault, Connie wondered. Was her great sin not telling Sal of Corey's paternity? Did Connie start their marriage with a lie? Is everything, all of this La Sangre madness, her own fault?

Sal, with Connie, and six-year-old Corey in tow, had moved to La Sangre from Fresno as the replacement Pastor for the La Sangre Christian Church's beloved, longtime, aging pastor. Sal and Connie certainly performed well as the handsome Christian couple, with a beautiful Christian boy. That performance went on successfully for eleven years, nary a wrinkle.

But The Great Satori Show was abruptly unplugged when Peter Freeman happened to arrive in town, jump-starting the bottled passions within the Satori family and La Sangre in general. People started doing strange things. Sal had a wild one-hour affair with the seriously traumatized Jessie Malana, who reacted by attempting to kill Corey but killing Peter Freeman instead, and then killing herself.

Those horrendous events created an unexpected blessing for Sal and Connie; their marriage finally became one of true passion, trust, humor; no longer pretension, no longer the Christian Carousel they were bored with.

So many questions, multiplying exponentially. *Did* their marriage really become true passion? What kind of "true" passion could be born of adultery? *Did* she and Sal trade in pretension for misplaced passion? *Was* their marriage now built on Sal fantasizing about his one-time fling with Jessie, while Connie continued to relive her one-time fling with Peter? *Should* she have told Sal from the beginning who Corey's father was? *Should* she have told *Corey* who his real father was? *Was* everything that happened all her life Connie's fault, for starting the lie and living it all these years?

"STOP IT!" Connie cried out loud. "IT'S TOO MUCH!"

Corey jolted and turned to his mother, who was looking straight at the ocean. "It's too damned much, Corey," she repeated, softer.

Corey reached out and touched his mother's elbow. "I'm with you Mom, I'm home."

Even with Corey gone for a year, they never lost their bond and their unspoken understanding, and Connie knew he wanted to leave again, to get the hell out of La Sangre. After all, he had his own life to live, however enigmatic it was. Corey will stay long enough to sadly watch Sal get buried and then take off again, like he'd sadly watched Peter get buried, and then took off for nearly a year.

Connie kept looking at the ocean, as it seemed to tease her with the nonsense of her life. "It's all a bad joke," she stated as fact, not feeling. It was something everyone should know. A bad joke.

Corey knew what his mother meant, but he didn't know how to respond. So he concentrated on suppressing his instinct to call the Lawrence Freeman Produce dispatcher and request a long-haul, Bakersfield to Boston and all points in between on Interstate 70.

Nathan Steer continued to bathe in his well-deserved gloat—yes, gloat!—over what was now his time. He reviewed it again: he and Julie *just happened* to be driving north on Highway One on Father's Day last year; okay, that was happenstance. He was in the right place at the right time, sure, he'll admit to that. Nathan then submitted the news of the deaths to the AP wire service. Okay, he was fast and diligent, again so what?

But Nathan didn't stop there, did he? He'd forged ahead, in between writing fluff pieces for the *Santa Rosa Dispatch* about what's-happening-in-Sonoma-County-this-weekend. Of course he didn't quit his job with the *Dispatch,* but he did encourage his wife to become friends with Lillian Walker, the new nurse at Santa Rosa General Hospital and long-time La Sangre resident. Nathan then purchased information about Jessie Malana from Ruby, the acknowledged town gossip, whom he continued to pay with cash and lobster meals at The Tides for any scrap of gossip that could aid in writing his book.

Then Nathan encouraged Julie to buy a house in La Sangre and move in. On the coattails of Julie's natural friendliness toward people he made friends with the most important people in La Sangre: besides Lillian, he buddied up (so he thought) with Matthew Grant and Dr. Ralph Owen. Doyle Seeno, well, he wasn't important, just a loser grease-monkey gas-pumper, but still a possible good source of information. Sal, Connie, and Corey, well they were just your typical dysfunctional Christian family, which of course became the foundation of his book.

Yes, Nathan's book, at long last, his *book*, which would definitely find a publisher now, what with not just one, but *two* La Sangre Father's Day murders in a row. For a moment he considered changing his title to *Father's Day In La Sangre*, but opted to stay with his original *The Secret Of La Sangre*; it was more intriguing, more provocative. It would jump at people out from any book store window.

Once Nathan and Julie settled into the La Sangre petri dish, he found his book writing itself. Nathan just went along with the flow, he and Julie attended church regularly (which Julie enjoyed), he was polite and proper, and asked a lot of intelligent and seemingly sincere questions about Christianity. A few tried to "save" him, of course, and he went along with it, going to church with Julie, and attending the men's Bible studies, where he managed to keep a straight face and steal observances when all heads were bowed in prayer.

Of course, there was also the financial benefit of the Steers' move to La Sangre, as any home and/or land on the California coast was a solid investment. Lillian had advised Julie that one of the La Sangre residents was ready to sell her small cottage and move into an assisted living facility in Santa Rosa. The old lady's house was perfect for Nathan and Julie, affordable due to its lack of an ocean view, sitting behind a larger house. The Steers managed to get a loan, what with Julie's strong RN salary with benefits, Nathan's much lower salary, and considerable help from her parents.

Julie walked in the front door, back from work, just as the phone rang.

"Hi babe!" he greeted her from the couch.

"Aren't you going to answer the phone?" Her voice had a harder edge than usual; she was exhausted from her 12-hour graveyard ER shift.

"Oh sure babe." Nathan picked up the phone as Julie went into the bedroom. "Hello?"

"Hello, Mr. Steer? This is Cindy Carlton of the San Francisco Literary Agency." She paused.

"Oh yes, Cindy Carlton!" Yes, Cindy Carlton, who wrote the rejection slip that is still taped to my desk. So, you've come crawling back. But on a Sunday? He was going to wait until Monday morning to call her. "And what can I do for you?" he asked, stifling his glee.

"Mr. Steer, I'm very sorry to bother you on a Sunday morning, but we would like to offer you an agent's contract to place your book, *Death Of A Football Player*, with a New York publisher. Three that we've talked to have shown interest, all major houses."

He knew better than to ask which publishers, that was her muscle in this transaction. But what surprised Nathan was that all this was happening on a Sunday, just hours after the event. Such is the power of the Associated Press, he guessed, to interrupt a writer agency's weekend plans, and apparently even their sleep.

"Well Miss Carlton, I've actually changed the title of my book to *The Secret Of La Sangre*." Nathan was no fool, he'll restrain his gloating and monitor his tone. The San Francisco Literary Agency was the best in town, and one of the best on the West Coast, and he wanted someone convenient to him, not down in Hollywood.

Julie heard Nathan's remarks and came out of the bedroom in her bra and half-slip. Nathan grinned at her with a thumbs-up.

"Oh yes," Cindy responded, ignoring his ill-contained snottiness. It was all part of agency work, putting up with the overblown egos of self-proclaimed writers. "Yes, I think that's a much better title. Let me outline the major points of our standard contract. Then I'll have a messenger drive it up to you. First of all, are you at the same address in Santa Rosa?"

"Oh no, my wife and I live in La Sangre now. We've lived here for almost a year."

Cindy Carlton was stunned. He was *living* in La Sangre all this time? He was right there in the middle of it! What has he seen and heard since he sent his last, weak manuscript to her? What more does he know?

Nathan kept silent since she held the ball.

"Well," Cindy ventured forth, "I want to say first of all, Mr. Steer..."

"Nathan's fine."

"Nathan, thank you, and please call me Cindy. First of all, we are pushing your book to the front, trying to get it in print by next month."

"NEXT MONTH?" Nathan blew it; he could no longer contain his excitement. Was this really happening? So much for playing coy! He looked at Julie, who widened her eyes, understanding what it all meant.

"Believe me, Nathan" Cindy continued, "we can do it. And while you're updating your book to include today's, uh, incident, we're at your disposal for any additional research you may need."

"Now Cindy, this is *my* book, right?"

"Of *course* it is, but what I'm saying is we've got researchers available for any leg work:

gathering the police reports, background checks, all that stuff, as well as transcribers so that you can just dictate into the telephone if you want to. We've got messengers at your disposal. This isn't just fast track, Nathan, this is lightning track."

"Lightning track," Nathan repeated softly. Oh yeah. This *is* a wild ride.

"Yes," Cindy responded. She knew she had him. "Now, I'm just going to outline the major points of the contract with you, but you should read it in depth, and if you want a lawyer to look at it, of course do so, but remember, every minute counts. Get a pen if you want to take notes. Oh, and when the messenger delivers the contract, he'll pick up a copy of the manuscript you had submitted to us last year. We'll get it entered into the word processor and go from there. Now, ready to take notes?"

Nathan beamed at Julie after he hung up. She had sat down on the couch, still half-dressed, uncertain how she felt about what was happening in front of her. Of course she only heard his side of the conversation, but somehow she didn't like what she heard.

"Every dog has his day, Jules! Come on baby, let's do it."

Julie stared at him.

"Hey Jules, come on! What's wrong?"

Julie couldn't stop staring at her husband. What's *wrong*, he had asked her? He knew she was always too tired right after work, and with everything else going on. Sal Satori, Connie's husband, is dead. That's what's wrong. Does that matter to you? "Oh, Nathan," she attempted, "I'm so tired...."

"Oh Jules, I know you always are after your shift, but," he looked towards the bedroom, "I'll do most of the work, all right?" His eyes were wide, his smile...ravenous.

Good Lord, there are suddenly two worlds in this living room, Julie realized. What world was her husband living in that I didn't know about until now?

You've had plenty of glimpses of it, Julie. Don't play dumb, and certainly don't play victim.

She managed a nod and got up from the couch and went into the bedroom, unhooking her bra.

"All riiiiight!" Nathan jumped up and followed her in.

FIVE

Connie was tending to Freeman when the phone rang. Corey wasn't at home, he'd gone to see Dr. Owen about possibly saying something at this morning's Sunday service, which she already decided she wasn't attending.

She didn't want to answer the phone, but didn't want to wake Grace either, who had arrived at 4 AM after driving all the way from Bakersfield after Connie's unashamed request last night. But then she heard Grace grab the extension in the guest room.

"Hello?"

"Hello, Mrs. Satori?"

"No, this is Grace, her friend." She and Connie had long agreed (and laughed about) that there was no way Grace would ever identify herself as "The mother of the football star with whom Connie begat Corey in high school." Besides, Connie and Grace had become, in fact, best friends, so that was that.

The caller identified himself as Pastor William Farrow, of the District Office in San

Francisco. The Office Secretary had heard the news and called Pastor Farrow directly. He immediately left for La Sangre to handle the Sunday morning service.

"Oh," Grace was relieved. "Yes, of course. Now the service is at ten, will you make it in time?"

"Yes, I'm already halfway there, I just stopped for gas. I didn't want to call too early." He paused. "How is Mrs. Satori, would she want to talk to me?"

"No, not now Mr. Farrow. Is there something I can help you with?"

"Well, I have an appropriate short message prepared for this morning's service, one I often use for pastors. Now, this isn't officially Pastor Satori's funeral, of course, but is there anyone in the congregation you think would like to speak this morning? We have to acknowledge what happened, we can't ignore it."

"Oh, yes, their son Corey agreed to preach, unless you think..."

"Oh no, that's a good idea, if he's willing to do that, good. I'll just stay in the back."

"Also, Matthew Grant and Dr. Owen, Sal's best friends here in town, will want to say something."

"Oh, that's good. I'll be staying around for a few days, I'm getting a room at the Santa Rosa Inn, I guess it's now the Flamingo, on old

Redwood Highway. I can take care of the funeral, when Mrs. Satori is ready to talk about it."

"Yes, yes, I'll tell her. Thank you."

"So I should be there at the church today by 9:00."

"Well don't come north from Bodega Bay. We've been told it's clogged with people trying to get here to snoop. You know, I didn't think about that until just now, but all those people will try to get into the service."

"Don't worry, I'll handle that. I'll man the door, and tell everyone it's for family and townspeople only."

"Good, thank you. Anyway, come straight out from Santa Rosa. Tell the police on Highway One who you are, they'll wave you through, like they did for me. I'll look out for you."

"Hello, Madge?" Ruby half-whispered into the phone at 9 AM. "I'm sorry, did I wake you?"

"Ruby? Is that you? Are you all right? Honey, what the *hell* is going on out there? Sam and I are watching the news. I'm sorry Honey, but that place you live in is sick!"

"I know, and yes, I'm all right," Ruby continued whispering.

"Speak up Honey!"

Ruby cleared her throat. "I know it's Sunday, but can you take me as an emergency?"

Madge quickly ransacked, she already had

a perm scheduled for Blanche at 2 PM. (She'll overlap Ruby so they can both see what color Blanche decides on this month.) "Oh, sure Honey, three all right?"

"Yes, three, I'll be there."

"And Ruby, if it's awful out there, I mean really awful, why don't you bring an overnight bag and spend the night here, in the guest room. Sam won't mind..." Madge reconsidered it, but it was too late. "Well, for one night anyway." Sam hated not being able to walk around in his boxers.

"No Madge, no, I have to stay here. They're all asking me, all of us, questions, the same questions over and over. I'm scared."

"What kind of questions?"

"I'll tell you when I get there."

Today was certainly going to be a newsy day in Madge's garage! "All right Honey. We'll see you at three. Your usual henna rinse?"

"No Madge, no! I want to go back to my natural color...whatever that is. I hope it's gray, I deserve it, after what I've done."

"What have you done Ruby?"

"I'll tell you when I get there."

The small La Sangre Christian Church was overflowing a half-hour before the service started, even though Pastor Farrow had properly weeded out non-residents and non-family. The service itself somehow went along neat and orderly. Even without the all the crying (much of it overacted) it would have been hard to pray, impossible to reflect. Had Connie been there, her declaration that morning would have been validated: none of it made sense.

After Pastor Farrow's short and heartfelt sermon, Corey read his father Sal's favorite scripture, John 15:13: "Greater love hath no man than this, that a man lay down his life for his." That was all he was able to say. He appealed to Matthew, who immediately came forward, standing next to Corey. "This...this is a hard time for all of us," Matthew said quietly. "I'm glad Sal and I became friends. He was taken from us, from his family, from me, way too soon. There's not much we can say right now, unless..." Matthew looked at Ralph Owen, who was sitting in the second row with his wife, Anne, who daintily dabbed her eyes. Ralph came forward while Matthew reached for Corey's elbow to escort him down from the podium.

"No, please stay there, both of you," Ralph said, as he placed himself between the two. "I am alive today, but only because of Pastor Satori, who intervened, and sacrificed his own life to save mine. That's all I can say about that for now. The police currently are investigating, gathering details. But I just want you all to know what a great man Pastor Salvatore Satori was...

is." There was light murmuring from the congregation, probably speculation on what really happened.

Ralph looked at Doyle, seated in the third row of pews, across from Nathan and Julie. Ralph could see Doyle wanted to come up, to say something. After all, it was Sal who gave Doyle the job at the gas station 11 years ago; it was Sal who gave Doyle the room over the garage, free meals at the Saloon, made him feel welcomed and needed, even if everyone else in town considered Doyle the village idiot. And it was Sal who encouraged Doyle to go into therapy with Dr. Owen.

"Doyle, come up here," Ralph said. "I know you'd like to share something. We"ll stand here with you."

Doyle, his cheeks tear-stained, hesitated, then rose and walked down the aisle tenuously, as if at any second he might turn around. It was exactly a year ago, that horrible Father's Day when Jessie Malana killed the football player and then herself, that Doyle confidently walked to the front of the church and led everyone in The Lord's Prayer. Now, he didn't know what he'd do or say, but Matthew extended an arm to Doyle as he went up the two steps to the podium.

"I uh..." Doyle stopped, looking at Ralph.

"Tell them what Pastor Satori did for you," Ralph encouraged.

"He..." Doyle looked at Ralph and then turned to the congregation. "I was a lonely, hurting man when I came here as a 38-year-old. Before that I'd spent twenty years wandering, doing self-taught auto-mechanic work through the Southwest. Pastor Satori...Sal...gave me a home, made me feel needed and even...special. He gave me a new life." Doyle choked. "They say that a boy, a young man, doesn't fully reach his manhood until his father dies, and now..." he turned to Ralph, who nodded encouragement. "And now, finally, I'm a man. Thank you Pastor Salvatore Satori."

After Pastor Farrow kindly greeted everyone as they exited the church, mitigating any questions by repeating "The police are investigating that," he went to the Satori home and knocked softly.

Grace opened the door. "Hello Pastor Farrow," she half-whispered. "Come in."

"Hi Grace," his tone matched hers. "How's Connie doing?"

"I think it was wise she didn't attend," she said as she shut the door behind him. "I'm sure she'll go to Sal's funeral, next week I guess."

"We can discuss that when she's ready."

Grace shook her head. "You might have to deal with me and Corey on all the arrangements."

"Of course." Pastor Farrow looked toward

the stairs. "Do you think I could talk to her now, just to pay my respects?"

Grace thought about it. "Yes. Yes, let's both go up. She's in bed, we won't stay long." Farrow followed Grace up the stairs.

Connie was sitting up in bed, watching Freeman in his playpen, which Corey had moved into his parents' bedroom. Grace and Corey agreed it was good therapy, it kept her focused.

Connie didn't look up as Pastor Farrow and Grace came just inside the open door. She knew Farrow pretty well, he was a guest speaker at their church a few times. Refreshingly, he wasn't one of those pompous, religious types, he was down to earth and she actually liked him. But she didn't want to speak with him, not now. Grace and Corey and Freeman were all she needed; and Lillian and Matthew, and maybe Ralph, as long as he didn't get too shrinky with her. Julie Steer? Connie liked her okay, but already had decided she didn't like or trust her husband Nathan. Anne Owen, Ralph's wife? No way. She was a fool, and not a harmless one. And what about Ruby, and Mary, and all the other La Sangre women? She told Grace to just keep them away.

"Connie," Pastor Farrow ventured, "I just wanted to see you for a minute, pay my respects."

Connie frowned and then nodded, still not looking at him.

"I...." He looked at Grace. "I told Grace that we can talk about the funeral later, when you're ready."

"I'll never be ready Deacon Farrow." The use of his official church title and surname was pointed. They were long on a first name basis.

Farrow ignored the barb. "I understand."

Do you? Connie wondered, taking her eyes off Freeman and looking at Farrow. Do you people ever really understand anything? You say you do but you don't. And I'm going to tell you so, even though it may not be true for you. I just want to have my say.

"Pastor Farrow, I don't want to hear about how God has a plan, and how all things work out for the good. Please, no religious talk."

William Farrow was taken aback, but only slightly. It wasn't such an unusual reaction to grief, and it was a legitimate feeling. Connie was just being more honest than most. Moreover, Farrow knew he had answered his phone this morning, gotten the news, driven up from San Francisco and without missing a beat, replaced her husband. How else could she respond? "Of course not, Connie...." he began.

"Mrs. Sal Satori," she corrected him, not without hostility.

"Mrs. Satori," he nodded in deference. "I just want you to know that you don't have to concern yourself at all with the church, nothing. One of the your ladies here in town, Mary, will handle piano duties, she did so this morning. I'm going to handle everything else in the interim."

"And when does that 'interim' end, Deacon Farrow? A week? A month? A year? A LIFETIME?" She coughed, a reaction to not having used her full voice in hours, and not having slept.

Farrow didn't react to her explosion. "It's okay Connie, stay with your grief, don't try to lock it up." He winced inside. Ouch, that was bad.

"Okay," Connie said plainly, not caring one way or the other whether what he said was appropriate or comforting. She didn't care if he meant well. It was all just words.

"Mrs. Freeman...Grace...knows how to get hold of me," he turned to her. Grace nodded.

Connie looked outside the bedroom window at the ocean. "Okay," she said again.

"I'll be at the church for a while today," Farrow said, "getting my bearings. Then I have to drive to San Rafael. My wife Elizabeth—you know her—will come up from the city this afternoon, she's taking the ferry over to San Rafael where I'll pick her up." Oh brother, what did all *that* stuff matter? He was seriously blowing it. Something he and Elizabeth always agreed upon was that women were better at this than men. But he was at least wise enough not to say to Connie "I'm praying for you." Instead he asked, "Would you like Elizabeth and me to stop by later today?"

Connie's airy "Oh if you want to" clearly meant No. Connie turned her attention back to Freeman, who was lying on his back in the play-pen, happily reaching for the colorful evasive mobiles hanging overhead.

Madge removed the hair dryer from Ruby's head, gave her hair a few finger-fluffs, and they both looked in the mirror.

"It makes you look..." Madge, always ready with false compliments, was at a loss.

"'Old' is the word I think," Ruby said with a strange, new sense of candor and self-depreca-tion. "That's just about the ugliest gray hair I've ever seen."

"Well Honey, you asked for it," Madge re-torted. "Now, Ruby, will you tell me what this is all about? Does it have something to do with that crazy town I've been telling you to move out of?"

Ruby shook her head, looking at the sad old lady reflected in the oval mirror. Madge, standing behind her, all made up and perfectly coiffed, could have passed for her daughter...no, her younger sister.

"Just *tell* me Ruby! What's this all about?"

Ruby looked at Madge through the mirror.

"All right, I'll tell you. I'm going to be a nun!"

Father's Day in La Sangre, California, finally and mercifully ended, the day sinking into the ocean along with the sun. Although the morbid sightseers had diminished somewhat, the police were still vigilant along Highway One to maintain traffic flow. The townspeople knocked on each others' doors to learn anything new, and took food to Connie's door.

"Oh thank you," Grace greeted them all kindly. "I'm Connie's friend, Grace. I'm sorry I couldn't come to church today. I thought it better if I stayed with Connie."

"Oh of course. May I..." they would all ask, looking past Grace to the living room and stairs.

Grace would smile and shake her head gently. "I'm sorry. It's not a good time."

"I understand," they all said. "Please tell her we're praying for her."

Unable to sleep, Corey lay in his old bedroom in his parents' house, not wanting to be there, not belonging there. Even with his mother, his baby brother, and his Grandma Grace here, he was a stranger. Maybe being in the room he grew up in, and his mother not changing anything in it, the San Francisco 49ers poster showing Pete Freeman front and center, was messing with his mind. Who the hell was he? First there was Corey the happy kid, then Corey who dropped out of college to be a trucker, then Corey the whoreson who turned into a whoremonger, and now some older, unhappy version of Corey, all alone in the world and all of eighteen years old.

He wondered if sleeping in his room above the garage, that Doyle had kept clean for him while he was away, would be any better. No, he couldn't do that; he'd slept in that room just one night, that last night, a year ago, with his father Pete.

What Corey really wanted to do was go sleep in his rig, which was still at the Santa Rosa Truck Stop. After church this morning he'd called dispatch at Lawrence Freeman Produce and explained that his Dad just died, and he'd left his rig and trailer at the Santa Rosa Truck Stop. The dispatcher had certainly seen the news but didn't know Corey's familial connection. He just offered his condolences and told Corey to meet a fellow driver there Monday morning to change out rigs so the load could get to Eureka in time.

Now Corey was lying in his bed, on his back, eyes open. So now what? Prepare for the funeral on Thursday? Repeat what he'd already said this morning, graciously accept the well-meant respects from the townspeople? None of that crap was any good. He needed to escape. But first, some sleep would be nice.

Sleep Corey.

"Corey." Sal was standing at the left side of the bed. "Everything's okay, it's really all right, Son."

"No Dad." He realized he was calling Sal "Dad" again. No more of this "Step-Dad" for Sal Satori and "Bio-Dad" for Pete Freeman. "No Dad, it's not all right. It'll never be all right. I don't like what God is doing. It's not fair. I feel like He's punishing me. I wandered, and now I can't get back."

Sal nodded and smiled. "It's your feeling, Corey, and that's okay, but it's not a Truth. But Son, listen," he placed a hand on Corey's chest, "you'll be able to handle everything that's coming to you. I know it's a tall order, God knows it is, but you can do it." He paused. "Your mother told you that I boxed as a kid, didn't she?"

Corey nodded. "It was the first thing she said, after we found out that it was you lying below the cliff. 'Your father boxed as a kid,' Mom told me. Why did she tell me that, right then? Why didn't *you* ever tell me?"

Sal smiled. "Corey, your Mom told you that right then to let you know I was a good boxer, a fighter, and I was good because I used my head. Those other guys would come out swinging wild, not planning, and all I had to do was watch them, move around them, give them a few fakes that they fell for and then gave me my opening. I always knocked them on their asses."

Corey's chuckle turned into tears. He grabbed his father's hand on his chest. "Oh Dad," he sobbed, "will you stay with me?"

"Of course I will. Maybe not always like this, but sure, I'll be with you." Sal looked across the bed.

"So will I Corey!" said a cheery, familiar voice.

Corey turned and saw Peter Freeman standing on the right side of the bed. He was in his red 49er uniform, holding his helmet. "Pete! Pete! It's really you! I was waiting to see you again!"

"I'm here, just like your other Dad." Pete smiled and nodded to Sal. "You know Corey, some boys don't even have one father, but you've got two!"

"Oh Dad," Corey turned back to Sal, "what am I going to do?"

"Well to start," Sal said, "first thing tomorrow you're going to go talk to Ralph."

"Dr. Owen?"

Sal looked over at Pete, who was now wearing his street clothes, as he was when Corey first met him.

"Yes Corey," Pete affirmed. "You're going to tell Dr. Owen exactly what led up to your Dad's death last night. Start with Maria, Bruno, all of that. Ralph needs to know it. He's got a lot of guilt going on right now, he needs some comforting too. And after you give him the information, he'll know what to do." Pete regarded Sal, who nodded in agreement.

Corey smiled and rolled onto his right side, waking up with Monday's rising sun.

MONDAY, JUNE 17, 1985

SIX

The Monday morning after Father's Day 1985 found La Sangre looking like a mix of Egypt, Sodom, and Gomorrah, with over half the one hundred townspeople planning to sell and move from this literally God-forsaken place. Their Pastor was dead, Satan had won, this was now his Evil Dominion.

On Highway One, realtors and investors from all over the Bay Area descended upon La Sangre, and they were as bad as the media. They swooped in like carpetbaggers, with buy-low, sell-high in their hearts. The police managed to hold them back, while a few of the more aggressive realtors shouted to a couple of the residents as they drove out to work, "Hey, we'll buy your house for $300,000! No fees, no repairs, no cleanup, no nothing! $300,000 cash!"

Financially, it was a safe offer, and a good one for both sides. All the homes were similar: two-bedroom, one-bath, wood-shingled, no foundations, charming though inefficient against the cold sea air. They all shared the same well, all had electricity and septic tanks, but many still only heated with wood stoves, legally grandfathered past the California Coastal Commission's Building Codes. The CCC morally couldn't make La Sangre wood-stovers comply with the increasing number of high-smog/no-burn days up and down the Pacific Coast.

In the meantime, the CCC did mandate that new La Sangre buyers purchase and use propane tanks for heating. The original owners with their wood stoves had always borne the responsibility of sparking a fire on their or their neighbors' wood-shingled roofs; but the nightly fog was a natural retardant, and thankfully a fire never lit. Only a few of the long-term owners carried fire or theft insurance.

While no one could deny La Sangre's considerable charm on Highway One, and its history as a 1910 village built as affordable spillover residences for Bodega Bay fishermen, it was now more famous as the town where NFL star Pete Freeman was murdered. In fact, Wine Country travel brochures now included a photo of the town, with a caption that simply read "La Sangre." America, and much of the world, knew of La Sangre only by what happened there, like they knew of Chappaquiddick, Massachusetts, sixteen years earlier. But charming or not, notorious or not, the CCC still wanted to get rid of "that hamlet of wooden shacks," and just turn it into a scenic Vista Point, with restrooms.

So who were all these potential La Sangre buyers, money in hand? They had been making offers since Pete Freeman was killed there last year, though nothing like $300,000. But now the ante was upped by this second year of deaths and suicides. The realtors all knew that the wealthy New Agers, spiritualists, Satan worshipers and Wiccans would easily pay a half-million to live within the allegedly evil environment that was known as La Sangre, which everyone now knew was Spanish for "The Blood."

Personal and religious beliefs aside, pro-Christian or anti-Christian, everyone agreed that there was something definitely wrong with that town, it wasn't a one-time fluke, and so the buyers were lining up like for a horror film festival. Just like "Stepford Wives" had become a commonplace term in the mid-1970's, so was "La Sangre Christians" becoming one in the mid-1980s. The town and its environment were considered fertile ground from which humans could draw some kind of power or magic. Of course, the Christians thought it was Satan's presence, pure and simple, but for others it was a powerfully electromagnetic combination of mystery, intrigue, and darkness. This is what Corey had learned at Sex Addicts Anonymous. There's always one more moment of sheer bliss, one more powerful and longer-lasting than the last one.

For those so driven in their spiritual drive, La Sangre promised the Final Cosmic Orgasm.

At daybreak Monday morning, Corey walked down the path to the Owens' cottage.

"Hey Corey," the Owens' next door neighbor appeared from his house, carrying a fully-packed box and placing it in the bed of his small pickup. "Sorry we have to leave, but we can't stay here no more."

"I know Burt, I understand."

"Your father gave his life for La Sangre, you know that Corey?"

"Yeah Burt, I know. Thank you." Burt had used those same words to Corey yesterday after the Sunday service. Corey knew that while Burt and everyone else all meant well, such remarks were like sympathy cards. All you do is just look at the signature and try to appreciate that the sender went to the trouble, stamp and all.

"Burt!" Mary called from inside. "You'll have to get the get the box of kitchen stuff, it's too heavy for me! Let's get going! I'm not going to spend another night in this hell-hole!"

Corey nodded dismissal to Burt and kept walking to the Owens' cottage. Oh all right, maybe La Sangre was still essentially good, however naive it was to believe that it was Satan himself who was destroying the town. Corey's dream last night with Sal and Pete put him on a more positive path, and if it meant staying and fighting whatever it was that had hold of the town, he would, like David battling Goliath.

"Hi Corey!" Ralph was surprised by his visit so early in the morning. He was still in his pajamas and bathrobe.

"I'm sorry Dr. Owen," Corey's head was half-down.

"No Corey!" Ralph almost said "No, Son," but that would be inappropriate so soon, if ever. This boy has just lost two fathers a year apart. "No, of course not, come on in. I'll get some coffee on, we'll go in my office. Mind if I get dressed?"

"Oh sure," Corey chuckled. "I can't stay too long. Doyle's driving me to the Santa Rosa Truck Stop so I can switch out rigs with another driver."

"Well, go on into my office, it's the room with the open door, on the right. I'll put on the coffee and join you in a minute," he went into the kitchen. "Or would you rather have orange juice?"

"No, coffee's fine. Dr. Owen?"

"Yes?"

"I want to tell you everything."

Ralph turned and looked at Corey. "Good."

Once Ralph and Corey were settled, their

coffee mugs on the small table between them, rather than Ralph giving his standard palms-up/what's-up gesture, he started by asking "You doing all right?"

Corey nodded, then shook his head.

Ralph nodded in understanding. "And your Mom?"

"Not so good. But Grace is there. She's going to stay for awhile."

"That's good," Ralph said. "I'm keeping an eye on your Mom. Last night, after we found out that...that it was your Dad," he paused respectfully and took a deep breath, "I asked your Mom if she wanted a mild sedative, she said no, which is fine. I'll watch out for depression, beyond the grief I mean, and we'll take it from there. She strikes me as a tough lady, though, underneath it all."

"Well, we'll see." Corey realized he hadn't yet made eye contact with Dr. Owen. He made himself look up. "Well, Dr. Owen..."

Ralph didn't ask Corey to call him Ralph. Corey had called him Dr. Owen all his young life, and he was still young and a certain amount of respect was in order, even with what Corey was going through. Ralph just nodded.

"Well," Corey said again, "I guess I'm the only one who really knows the so-called 'secret' of La Sangre."

Of all Dr. Owen's many patients' confessions,

this one required the greatest amount of self-restraint and impartial expression. His facial muscles were going to get a morning workout, that was for sure. Maybe he should have put some sugar into his ordinarily black coffee.

Ruby, now gray-haired and without her poofy 'do, rummaged through her closet, gathering her too-low-cut blouses, push-up bras, too-bright-for-church colors, and negligees that she purposely wore with the window shades up. She shoved them all into a Glad Trash Bag.

"I will not flirt with men," she vowed in rhythm while shoving items in the trash bag. "I will wear black, even sack cloth if I have to."

She suddenly stopped.

"You will never forgive me, will you Lord?"

She waited. In her lost heart she was certain He would not. He said nothing. He didn't love her anymore. Even the ocean was quiet.

It took Corey 25 minutes to tell Ralph about meeting Maria Malana, having sex with her for two days, discovering the ruse, and about her horrid abuse from her father, which resulted in her sister/daughter Jessie.

Ralph managed to maintain a neutral expression, which was hard because while he'd long suspected Jessie as an incest victim, given all the sessions he spent with her, she never confessed it. "And," Ralph finally responded, "Maria believed that you were the one who had sex with Jessie, putting her on tilt?"

"At first, but she believed me when I denied it."

Ralph took in some air. "No matter how long I've been a shrink, Corey, child abuse never loses its stab in my heart. Even medical school can't prepare you for that. They teach us to be empathetic, but not to absorb the patients' pain. That's easy in theory, but hard in practice."

Corey smiled. "I guess that's good. I mean, I guess that means even psychiatrists are human."

"Yeah Corey, we are. Most of us anyway." Ralph grabbed the coffee pot and refilled their mugs, giving himself a minute to make the decision of whether or not to tell Corey about.... dammit, the boy is 18, he's lost both his fathers, Sal had told Ralph about Peter Freeman being Corey's father, and about his tryst with Jessie in one of their many sessions/confessionals. So Ralph decided he'd tell Corey, just like he'd told the police, exactly what happened the night before last.

"Corey, Saturday night at the cliff, Maria was there with that bodyguard of hers; she was shouting at me, accusing me of having sex with Jessie."

Corey's eyes widened.

"Corey, when your father heard that lie he

cried out to Maria, 'No, it wasn't Ralph, it was...' Bruno then lunged at me and Sal couldn't finish the sentence. Your Dad leaped and pushed me down and Bruno got him instead." Ralph leaned back in his chair and let Corey absorb what he said for a moment. "Corey, that was Sal who did that. My friend. Your father. He and I had become best friends over this past year, while you were gone. And I can say with authority that was pure Salvatore Satori to do what he did. He threw himself against me, knocking me away, and Bruno ended up shoving him off the cliff instead of me..." Ralph stopped.

Silence, until Corey spoke.

"My father did that?"

Ralph nodded sadly. "Yes, and I have to live with that, the good and the bad of it. Sal died for me, he died a hero. I know I said this at the service yesterday, but I didn't mention the details leading up to it."

"So my father was going to say 'It wasn't Ralph, it was *me* who had sex with Jessie.' That's the detail you avoided, right?"

Ralph nodded, maintaining eye contact with Corey. "Yes. Your Dad had only the one time with Jessie, the night before Pete was killed, but it was enough to unhinge her. Maria knew that about Jessie, it was the same for herself, as you found out."

"That Father's Day, last year, when I was

crossing the road to my...to both of my fathers, Jessie pointed her car right at me. I saw her face through the windshield for just one second, it was...it was...." Corey remembered the painting Maria had done of him during their two mad days together at Wadell Beach. "It was like Maria's face," Corey continued, "it was evil."

Ralph nodded. Evil was a theological term, of course, not a psychiatric one. While Ralph certainly had his share of religious patients, he always steered them towards their own behavior and away from a third-entity who could be responsible, be it God or the devil. "The devil made me do it" didn't fly in Ralph's office. But with Jessie—and apparently with Maria also—it certainly appeared that way.

"Yes," Ralph agreed softly, "I saw that evil too. I've seen a lot of hurt and pain in my work, but I never saw it so crystallized into evil as I saw with Jessie. I really thought she could grow, move past it. She worked her therapy, lived in our house by the ocean, prayed and studied her Bible, but she just couldn't do it."

There was a searching, liberating silence in Ralph's office.

Ralph finally took a deep breath; there was one last thing Corey needed to know. "Corey, your Father confessed his sin of adultery to your Mother, and I believe she forgave him."

Corey looked at Ralph. "I...I don't know just

what to do with that."

"It's a lot for an 18-year-old to hear," Ralph agreed, "and it was a hard decision for me to make, Corey, to tell you all this. I finally decided it was important that you know, as his son, how and why your Dad died. You as a Christian may believe he had to pay for his sin, I don't know about that, but for me, it's certainly the measure of a great man."

Corey heard everything and absorbed it all. "My father saved your life just like Peter Freeman saved mine," he finally said.

Ralph nodded, eyes down. "Both your fathers died the same way. They both gave their lives for someone else."

More silence.

"Ready to move on?" Ralph asked.

Corey nodded silently.

"Okay Corey," Ralph finally broke the gentle silence for his professional summation. "Now, instead of dealing with everyone's various behaviors, let's you and I map this out like lawyers. Let's look at the facts. One: Maria stalked you in Santa Cruz and trapped you because she thought you were the one who had sex with Jessie, and she chose to punish you in a very bizarre way. When you told her it wasn't you who was with Jessie, she believed you and deduced I must therefore be the one who did it, as Jessie's psychiatrist. Two: Maria told you about a spy she had in La Sangre, and we don't know who that is. Three: only Bruno and Maria knew of your relationship with Maria. Finally—and probably most important—Bruno, Maria and I were present at Sal's confession. Bruno is dead, and I'm not sure that Maria heard what Sal said, totally engulfed as she was in her rage."

"But Maria *might* have heard it?" Corey suggested.

Ralph nodded. "She might have. Now, there's someone else in this town who might know about your Father and Jessie."

"Who?"

"The same person in this town that Maria paid as a spy. Did this person offer Maria his or her suspicions about me as Jessie's therapist? Or, did this person actually know it was your father who had been with Jessie, and was he or she trying to extort Sal, threatening to ruin his name, his standing as a pastor?"

"I can't believe someone would want to do that."

"It happens, Corey. Non-believers love to crucify men of the cloth, just like repressed, angry people do with psychiatrists. We're the enemy. I'm sure it was Maria who filed the complaint against me with the California Psychiatric Association, claiming that I had sex with Jessie. They did an investigation and I was found not suspect. Again, we have no idea who this La

Sangre spy might be, who put such ideas into Maria's head, but I have my suspicions."

"Mary, the operator, who we had to go through when there were only a couple of homes with private lines..."

"Yeah, I got a private line when we first bought our home. Mrs. Owen says Mary's a real Mrs. Olesen."

Corey chuckled and nodded. "We all knew Mary used to listen in to our calls. My Mom and I didn't know it, but Dad..." Corey stumbled. "...Dad, had his own locked private line." Corey considered something. "But besides Mary there's someone else..."

"Ruby? Yeah, I'm thinking of her too. But the most important thing is that I want to respect Sal's memory. We don't know how much our two La Sangre suspects know, or what they plan to do with such information. Maybe nothing on either count, but Maria may need to use this information for legal reasons, that Sal had sex with Jessie."

"What? How?"

"Sal having sex with Jessie unhinged her and led her to attempted murder—against you in misplaced rage—and to her own suicide. Knowing this would help explain Maria's own out-of-control rage, the same rage Jessie had due to their connected abuse of incest. "

"So my father's affair with Jessie would have

to come out in court?"

Ralph looked at him. "The death penalty was abolished in California in 1972, but given what Maria's gone through, her life sentence might include the possibility of parole."

"How long a sentence?" Corey asked too quickly, too eagerly.

Ralph ignored it. "I don't know."

The grandfather clock in the living room chimed eight.

"I would be willing," Ralph said, "to speak of Maria's damaged psyche in a court of law. But I don't think I'm the person to present this to her, or to her lawyer, assuming she already got one. It would be better coming from someone she believes and, I think, actually trusts." Ralph finished and held Corey's gaze.

"Yeah," Corey looked upward, thoughtfully, "I do believe she trusts me, or *trusted* me."

"You came to Maria open-hearted, pure as the driven snow. But she was driven to tromp on it and make it dirty. Just like Jessie tried to run you over."

Corey looked down, then back up at Ralph. "I'll do it. I'll see Maria. I'll tell her about everything you've told me, that it could help her. If she does trust me, she'll listen to me." Corey looked toward the window, the morning sun getting brighter. "Just where is she?"

"Well, I know she was sent to the County

Jail, though they may be transporting her to Sacramento today. I can call my associate in the County and verify her location, and set up a visit for you."

Corey nodded, eyes firmly on Ralph.

"Meet and kill your dragon, Boy," Ralph told him.

"You mean kill my Goliath," Corey said.

SEVEN

Theresa Spagopolous was an exceptionally beautiful Greek American woman. Hollywood's best makeup artists wouldn't have known what to do with her. Her green eyes, oval face, lush black hair, and olive skin would have defied their attempts to mold her into their unimaginative market-geared conception of beauty. But that was all moot because Theresa was as smart as she was beautiful. Sure, she could have descended on Hollywood, confounding the starmakers and the public, but she would have left as abruptly as she arrived and not looked back. "Einai iii Greta Garbo," her Yaya would often comment about her favorite grandchild.

As a child in the family's Spago Brothers Greek Restaurant in Santa Rosa, Theresa slaved away before and after school, and was fine with it. Naturally disciplined, she knew she was refining her natural talents as she scrubbed, scraped, mopped, chopped and prepped. While she wouldn't be able to articulate it until she was into her late teens, she somehow knew that the humbling restaurant work was building her strength of character.

As a teenager, when Theresa started serving, ringing up the tabs and collecting payments (with huge tips), she just assumed her ability to determine how big a tip she'd be given was plain common sense. Families were always cheap, women were the worst; three or four of women together were deadly, sending her back umpteen times and deducting from their ten percent limit every perceived mistake she made, not to mention outright hostility to her beauty and grace, even in a waitress uniform. Two or more businessmen with credit cards were always a gold mine; they just wanted their food brought to them quickly, and to flirt with the waitress. Theresa obliged them with both. But the best tippers were men with a date. The man always played Big Spender, although his date didn't appreciate his gushing remarks to and about their waitress.

But it was more than common sense, Theresa soon realized, it was her keen insight. Theresa overheard conversations, understood what everyone's motives and expectations were. She knew how to make small talk with the customers, who would give her the information she needed to fill in the blanks, and by the end of their meal, she could write a dossier of the person who was now asking her for a coffee refill and a slice of

Mama Spagopolous' delectable baklava, the recipe handed down from antiquity.

By the time Theresa turned 18 and graduated from Santa Rosa High School (with honors), she ruled out psychiatry, the law, and certainly Hollywood as possible vocations, all three of which she would have naturally excelled at. Psychiatry and the law meant spending too much time in college and post-grad while life passed her by, and Hollywood to her was just one small step above prostitution.

Now at legal age, Theresa's brothers Constantine and Nicholas generously gave her a third of the restaurant's take, including the take-out bakery and the catering. At that point Theresa worked even harder, founding and organizing the annual Sonoma County Greek Festival, which closed down Fourth Street in Santa Rosa and drew people from as far as San Francisco, offering stiff competition to the famous annual Garlic Festival at Gilroy, south of San Jose. And all the while she heard from her Mama and Yaya: "Theresa you're such a beautiful and hard-working girl, you're healthy and could have as many children as you want. There are a lot of rich handsome Greek men who would make you a good husband!"

"Where are they Mama?"

"We find you one in San Francisco. At Holy Trinity Greek Orthodox Church in San

Francisco. Or maybe even find you a priest to marry, no?"

Sure Mama, sure Yaya, she'd falsely promise them. She liked men, but their superficiality and materialism bored her, while women annoyed her with their pettiness. She had no friends, and didn't date, not for lack of offers of both.

When Theresa turned 21, she surprised her family (and even surprised herself) by taking every dollar she'd earned and deposited into the bank since a child, and using it for a down payment on a well-worn two-bedroom home on the Old Redwood Highway, north of Santa Rosa. Dumbfounded as they were, her parents co-signed, knowing their daughter would always work, always make money...however to Mama's chagrin. Theresa had the house remodeled inside and out, the front yard landscaped, and she went to a sign maker.

Theresa by this time knew who she was and what she was, and the "what" part was always nameless. But she'll have to call it something, won't she? Psychic maybe? She shivered. They struck her as a bunch of mind readers, they could only see what the person already knew of themselves. Most psychics are clueless beyond that. Clairvoyant? That sounded better, but it was just like going from "maid" to "household technician." Well, she'll just advertise what she does, not what she is. She didn't have to think about her business name. It was the from Greek goddess of wisdom:

MADAME ATHENA
SPIRITUAL READINGS

When working she wore Liz Taylor/Cleopatra eye makeup, a golden robe, and a green turban that brought out the green in her olive skin, because that's what customers expected. She wore her best crucifix, used only at Christmas and Easter, to protect herself from negativity. She also leaned heavily on her Greek accent, which she had learned to control as a child. When in the restaurant or out in public she was herself, with no accent, no makeup and thick brown hair tied modestly behind her. Few in Santa Rosa were the wiser.

Madame Athena was in business for seven years, making good money with minimal effort and overhead, while showing up at Spago Brothers at 5 AM daily to help Mama bake. Once the breakfast rush was over and the lunch menu was prepped, she drove to her new home where she showered and donned her Madame Athena costume. She gave readings until 8 PM, and word of mouth kept her booked.

Theresa's brown hair turned completely white after a particularly challenging session for a new client, who suffered nonstop illness all her 23 years. "You *enjoy* being sick don't you?" she confronted the client. "You love the pain. You caress it, you stroke it like a dying cat. It brings you attention. Well this is your last chance: throw the cat out and let the poor thing die with dignity, and start living *your* life, *now*!" Whatever pain the client thought he had was immediately gone. He soon got a job and moved out of his parents' house.

Going white at 28 didn't bother Theresa. She accepted that all the knowledge and power that was swirling around in her head was a bit much for her scalp, and she didn't care. The white hair was as thick and beautiful as the brown was, offering an even more pleasing contrast to her darker skin tones, making Theresa further unrecognizable when in public, if no less entrancing.

Theresa's insight may have mystified her but it never scared her. She respected it and didn't abuse it; she could turn it on and off like a light switch. Without the gift evident in public, people were attracted to her exotic beauty and engaging personality. If they saw her professionally—turbaned, robed, and made up, with the "gift switch" on—they knew she was speaking their truth, while her looks were just a very nice accessory.

Theresa's family spent hours praying at the modest St. Constantine Greek Orthodox Church in Santa Rosa, that God would destroy the demon that was inside of their daughter.

"Papa, it comes from God," Theresa would implore. "It's a gift, like my brother Constantine always knows where the fish are!"

"They get that from me, their Papa! So what you do with this gift, iii kori mia?"

"I can help people, Papa. People are confused, they're lonely, they're afraid. I can help them."

Still, Papa and Mama started crossing themselves whenever Theresa's name was mentioned. Her Yaya, who never learned English in this New America, put garlic under Theresa's pillow, as if Theresa couldn't smell the cloves when she went to bed; she just sneaked them back into the kitchen. Up to her death, Yaya was certain that Theresa had been cursed by the devil, and God gave her the white hair as a sign of punishment.

So be it, Theresa shrugged, white hair and all. In the meantime, as Madame Athena she was making tons of money, and St. Constantine's Church certainly didn't reject her faithful attendance and generous tithes.

A few days before the second La Sangre/Father's Day tragedy of 1985, Theresa received a new client, a successful Sonoma County realtor, who asked The Madame for hot tips on the real estate market.

"I'm sorry, I can not and will not use my

vision for financial gain," Theresa told the realtor, not a little annoyed. If Theresa didn't hold onto her high morals, giving readings would put her on the same level as Hollywood.

"Well, is there *anything* you can tell me?" the aggressive, sharply dressed, realtor-with-an-attitude snapped at her.

Theresa looked at her, already receiving information. "I can give you a personal reading that may help you in your work, perhaps about discerning your potential buyers, what to look for in the sellers, and making the right decisions."

"Oh they teach us that stuff in real estate school!"

"Fine, do you want a reading or don't you? It's already fifty dollars for taking my time."

"Oh all right," the realtor sighed in disappointment. She had an open house in an hour for a top-end home in Healdsburg. "What can you tell me?"

Now, the day after the news of La Sangre, Theresa called the realtor at her office.

"Hello, Nancy? This is Madame Athena."

"Oh!" the realtor was surprised and lowered her voice. "Madame? Did you see something else? Another vision?"

"No, not for you, for me. I need you to find me a home in La Sangre, now."

"A rental? I don't think..."

"No, to purchase. I'll pay you double your usual fee if we can do this today."

Nancy was elated, her mind already calculating her approximate commission. "But in La Sangre, Madame? After what happened yesterday? Are...are you sure?"

"Yes, I'm sure, and my legal name is Theresa Spagopolous. You and I are realtor/buyer in this transaction, and I'll ask you to keep my professional name in confidence. The two are completely separate. Do you understand?"

"Uh...of course Madame...uh, Miss Spa...."

"Spa-*gop*-o-lus."

"Miss Spagopolous. Well you're in luck, there's already a vacant house there, just listed, it's..." She exaggerated some paper-rustling on her desk for the sound of urgency. "Oh, here it is...and. ..it's still available! I'd have thought it was already sold, what with all the New Agers looking for a home in La Sangre..." Oh shit. She was doing great until she used the potentially offensive term, New Ager. Nancy stopped, and tried to recover.

"That's all right, Nancy," Theresa sighed. Nancy The Realtor was the easiest read she ever had; Theresa feel like a thief taking her money. "Yes, I guess 'New Ager' includes me, fine. So, let's look at the house." They agreed to meet in La Sangre in one hour.

Nancy canceled the day's appointments and drove to La Sangre. From the news, the rubbernecking traffic to La Sangre was backing up. But she actually arrived in just 30 minutes, and had only three cars ahead of her trying to pass through La Sangre. She gave the young deputy her card and the house number she was going to show.

"All right ma'am, but," he looked at his watch, "you've got 30 minutes. Is that your buyer in the next car?"

Nancy looked in the rear view mirror. "No. She should be here any minute."

"All right, just park over there on the shoulder so she, and we, can see you. Then you two walk down together. No visitor vehicles allowed down there including yours. Don't knock on *anybody's* door. Understand?"

Nancy nodded, noticing that the deputy was studying her business card. "Are you interested in buying or selling anything?" she asked him professionally.

"On my salary? I still live with my parents."

By the time Corey left Ralph's office, Anne Owen was up and in the kitchen, updating her manuscript, *The Mystery Of La Sangre,* adding last night's murder. Ralph had just lost his best friend, and now his wife was pounding furiously on her electric typewriter, driven to sell a book.

The mad click-clicking of the keys and ching! of the return key made Ralph sick, so he put on a heavy jacket and took his coffee out to the front porch.

"Good morning Dr. Owen."

Ralph looked up. "Oh, hi Doyle. Have a seat."

"Well," Doyle looked around, "I need to talk."

"Oh sure. Let's go in to my office. The closed door will drown out my wife's writing frenzy."

"Writing?"

"Never mind, don't get me started."

Mrs. Owen's ominous key-pounding in the kitchen rattled through the entire cottage, but it wasn't too bad in Ralph's office, once the door was shut. "You must have noticed that sound-proof door before," he said to Doyle. "I had that put in so my clients know that our conversations can't be heard; but it has the reverse benefit too. We can't hear her so badly." Indeed, the type-writer clicking was muffled. Ralph settled in his chair opposite Doyle. "So, what's going on? Oh I'm sorry, coffee?"

"No I'm good. I had a dream last night."

"Oh no," Ralph said softly. "Of your child-hood again?"

"No, not that, not at all. Those are long gone. This one is good, I think. I was in 'The Wizard Of Oz,' when they come out of the forest and see the Emerald City. It was just like in the movie. It was green and beautiful."

"Were you one of the characters in the movie?" This wasn't the first time Ralph heard the Wizard of Oz dream from a patient. He always asked which character they were.

Doyle considered, then shook his head. "No, I was just me, by myself, looking at the Emerald City."

"How did you feel, looking at it?"

Doyle thought some more. "I wanted to go there."

"So, did you walk toward the city?"

The muffled typewriter clicking suddenly stopped, offering a beautiful silence.

"Ah, at last," Ralph sighed. "So, did you walk to the Emerald City?"

"No, I..."

The typing resumed.

Doyle and Ralph shared a humorous grimace.

"Dr. Owen," Doyle asked with a smile, "is Mrs. Owen transcribing everything I say?"

They laughed, while Ralph noted how Doyle's vocabulary was improving; previously he would have said "writing down" instead of "transcribing." Doyle was becoming more engaged with people and listening more, and likely reading more. He'll have to ask Doyle about that.

"So, what was the question?" Doyle asked, wiping his right eye with his wrist.

"Oh, sorry. So did you walk to the Emerald City?"

"Oh, yeah," Doyle smiled, remembering the beautiful dream. "No, I just stood there, but I wanted to go to it."

Ralph studied Doyle as he did when his own children were growing up. He saw a new man risen from the damaged child he'd been treating—at quite an accelerated rate, faster than any patient he'd ever had—for the past year. "So Doyle, it seems like you're ready to make some kind of decision. Do you know what it is?"

"I think I'm going to leave La Sangre," Doyle announced promptly.

Ralph nodded, happy with what he heard. "Yes, some people are leaving."

"But not for their reasons. Not just because Pastor Satori is dead." Doyle stopped and looked down. "It still doesn't seem real."

Doyle and Ralph shared the sadness for a few seconds. "No, it won't for a while," Ralph finally said. "I feel the same way. It's a natural reaction to shock, and it actually serves to protect us, to help us function and do what we have to do." Ralph thought for a moment. "But no, that's not always true. I really cracked up after Matt tossed that thug over the cliff with his car. You should have seen me, a babbling idiot. But for Matt slapping me across the face I might have jumped off the cliff too."

They both imagined the sight of it and broke into a new laughter.

"So, anyway," Ralph finally came down, "do you have any idea where you might move to? What you'll do?"

"I'm not thinking about that, yet. I just want to leave the La Sangre Last Chance Gas Station. When I started working there, I thought it really was my last chance, and it became my home. But now...I want to do something else."

"Do you know what?"

"No."

"You're a good mechanic, you enjoy it don't you?"

"I don't enjoy waiting a month for a car to work on, there aren't enough cars here. And any visitor who breaks down here just wants to get towed to the dealerships in Santa Rosa. They don't trust a tall skinny guy in a two-bit town, and I can't blame 'em. I just pump their gas. It's time to move on."

They were silent for a moment, Ralph studying Doyle warmly. It was time. "Doyle, do you remember what I did the first time we met here, in my office, instead of in Sal's..." Ralph's voice caught. "...office?"

Doyle shook his head. So much had happened with Dr. Owen this past year: fear, discovery, anger, the breakthrough, the tears.

"I measured you against the door jamb," Ralph pointed behind Doyle.

Doyle turned and looked. He could see the

pencil mark on the white trim. "Oh, yeah."

"Do you know why I did that?"

"I wondered about it, but I was too messed up to worry about it, too insecure to even ask a question."

"Well, I'd like to measure you again. Come on, put your back against the door jamb."

Doyle hesitated. A healthy reaction, Ralph noted. Doyle no longer did so easily what others, particularly authority figures, asked him to. He considered it first, and then made a decision. "Okay," Doyle said. He got up and stood with his back against the door, remembering with warmth his mother doing that in their kitchen as he grew. ("You're going to be taller than your Father!" she'd told Doyle with pride. He didn't believe it at the time.) Ralph grabbed a pencil from his desk and made the mark where the top of Doyle's head met the door. "There you go. Now, take a look."

Doyle turned and looked at the new mark. "Is that me?" With his mechanic/ruler eye, he saw it was one and 3/8 inch above the old one.

"It sure is," Ralph grinned. "You've grown up. Literally. You used to walk with your shoulders slumped, neck and back compressed, head down. Us shrinks refer to is as an 'apologetic posture.' Haven't you felt the difference lately?"

Doyle nodded, surprised. "When I...look in the mirror now, I think I notice it. It's a new..."

He stopped, remembering. ("What are you looking for?" Jay had asked him in the rest area bathroom.)

Ralph knew Doyle couldn't finish the statement, he just needs a push, a shove if necessary. Now is the time. "Are you still going to your addiction meetings?" he asked Doyle.

"Not so much, not every week."

"Is there a reason for that?"

Doyle had to think about it; he looked down. He looked back up at Ralph. "There's nothing for me at the book stores or rest areas; it's a big waste of time, and it can ruin my day."

"And if you did go to those places, how would your day be ruined?"

"I'm...I'm having too much fun now being me to go to those places, and I'd rather be me than not me. The last time I tried to go to the Santa Rosa Adult Book Store I saw Corey's car parked there..." Doyle stopped, embarrassed with the accidental disclosure. "Oh, sorry..."

Ralph just gave a closed-eyed nod. Corey had already told him of his wild life.

"And," Doyle continued, "I thought, 'This isn't him.' And I knew that this isn't me, either. I turned around and haven't been back."

"Did you hear what you said, your first sentence?"

Doyle shook his head. Dr. Owen was sure slamming him today.

"You said you're having too much fun being...?"

Doyle smiled sheepishly. "Too much fun being me. Or..." Doyle looked up at the painting on the wall, a man watering a horse at a pond, like he did back in Texas. He'd almost forgotten about his old mare, Bitsy. He looked back at Ralph. "I've gone back to the *original* me, the real me."

Ralph nodded and smiled, eyes barely watering. This why he was a shrink, and a damned good one at that. Worth every penny he didn't earn from Doyle.

"Doyle, it's time you started living your life. So, get the hell out of my office. You've graduated."

Doyle burst into his third laughter in their short, and last, session. Ralph joined him, tears flowing. He wasn't sure if Doyle would think his tears were of laughter, or of the combined effect of Doyle's rebirth and Ralph's attaining full appreciation of his own self. Ralph hoped it was the latter, but it didn't matter. All Ralph knew was that he was going to miss Doyle.

As Theresa drove from Santa Rosa to meet Nancy at La Sangre, she hoped the always pleasant drive would help focus her sudden urge to buy a home there. Yes, it was her gift that brought it on, she knew that much, but what could she do in La Sangre that she couldn't do at her home office on the Old Redwood Highway? Why is she being told to buy a home there? Is this some kind of spiritual battle, like one of those possession movies? Was she being called there to fight that inherent evil some people believe is at the core of the deaths and suicides in that place?

Come on, "Madame Athena," are going to be a strong Greek woman, or are you going to be a sissy-girl the way your older brothers would taunt you when you were little? ("Aw, come on Terri, don't be a sissy-girl!") And indeed, thanks to Theresa's two wonderful brothers, she wasn't a sissy-girl, and she could probably whip both their butts if she had to, and they both knew it.

Well okay, the reason she's being called to La Sangre is a mystery, she'll just have to follow it and see what happens. Certainly if she's being called into spiritual warfare there, it wouldn't surprise her, it could even be exciting. After all, she's been through that town a few times—everybody's been there due to it being on Highway One—and she even ate in the La Sangre Saloon once. She remembered the pretty-but-hard-faced blonde waitress who was clearly damaged; Theresa saw it and, after the first La Sangre accident, she put it together that that waitress was Jessie Malana, who drove off the cliff. But by the time Theresa saw her, she knew there was nothing she could do. She couldn't take the waitress aside and tell her, "There's something important you need to know. I'm a psychic, I can give you a free reading." Theresa had long given up trying to help people unless they asked for it. And even then Theresa just gave them the information, the rest was their responsibility, not hers.

Theresa sighed and decided that this powerful draw of La Sangre will be an adventure, something new and different and challenging. Yes, that was it! She was going to meet a personal challenge! Something new in her life! "Go Terri go!" her brothers would shout playing softball when she got a solid hit and ran to first base, and rounded it to second.

Okay then, go Theresa go, to La Sangre.

She made the left turn onto Highway One, and drove as far as the La Sangre Christian Church on the right, where she stopped behind two vehicles; a young deputy was questioning the front one. The realtor had warned her about this probable delay, but the sightseers must have slimmed down since yesterday, Theresa reckoned. But they'll probably be back en masse come the weekend.

Theresa looked at the church, where she saw a tall, thin middle-aged man sitting on the steps, crying; an even taller, bigger, red-bearded man was seated next to him, his arm around the thin man's shoulders. An Irish Setter was on the other side of the thin man; the big man and the dog were pressing in against him, protecting him. It was a vision of course, but this particular one was definitely from the not-so-distant past, not the future. She knew that much.

"Move up please!" the deputy raised his voice. The two cars before her had driven on while she was still studying the vision, considering the details. She put her car in gear and pulled up even with the young deputy—he still lives with his parents and can't afford a first-and-last month's rent to get a place of his own—and let down her passenger window.

"Driving straight through towards Bodega Bay, ma'am?" the deputy asked. (His girlfriend is pressuring him to move from his parents' home and get a place for the two of them. "You can certainly afford splitting the rent!" the girlfriend said shrilly. He hasn't even asked her to marry him and she's already nagging.)

STOP IT! Theresa let her inner voice yell as loud as she dared. "No officer, I'm stopping in La Sangre."

"Are you a resident?"

"No."

"You have business in La Sangre?"

"Yes. I'm meeting a realtor, Nancy Rappolt of North Home Realty, to look at a house I may buy."

"Oh yeah, she's already here, waiting for you." The deputy pointed to Nancy's car parked ahead on the shoulder. "Go ahead, leave your car where hers is. She'll walk you down to the house."

"Thank you." Theresa nodded (Whatever you do, Deputy, don't move in with that girl!) and drove on.

Yes, it was just like her previous visits to La Sangre: her gift was kicking in without her consent, and she didn't like it.

Oh you'll get used to it, "Madame Athena."

Theresa couldn't be sure if that was God encouraging her, or maybe it was the enemy. That was new too. It was always just her and God, no interference. But still, this voice was good-natured, like Constantine and Nicholas when they bragged that they tormented Theresa for her own good, especially when dealing with people, and men in particular. Her brothers weren't wrong. But the devil can have a pleasant countenance, too.

Okay, okay, she tried to finalize it all. If she was here to do battle, with some inner or outer enemy, she'll do it. Amen.

But instead of stopping at the dirt road where Nancy was parked, Theresa found herself proceeding to the Last Chance Gas Station, on the left. She didn't notice Nancy watching from the shoulder, who just figured that Theresa needed gas.

But Theresa didn't need gas. She was doing what she was told to do.

Doyle left Ralph's home conscious of his new walk, and feeling 20 pounds lighter. He must have been that way for a while and not noticed it. When he got to the dirt road leading up to the One he became self-conscious, wondering if he now looked like those obnoxious, albeit good-natured boys back in Texas, thrusting their chests out and over-swinging their arms. But by the time Doyle reached the One he relaxed into it and looked and felt more natural about it. He stopped at the One and waited for a car to pass from the north before he crossed. They were driving under the 15 mph speed limit, if that was possible, marking themselves as rubberneckers. They stopped for Doyle, and the driver waved him on. Doyle shook his head and held his ground.

The car's passenger wanted to know who this tall, slim, not-bad-looking, confident man was, and what piece of the La Sangre puzzle he might be. She stuck her head out the window.

"Who are you?" she asked. "Do you live here?"

Doyle met her gaze and didn't move. I am Doyle Seeno, he answered her question silently and resolutely. I was born and raised in Texas. In fact, I'm an Italian Texan, if you need to pigeonhole me. And, I am a good mechanic. La Sangre is my home, but not for much longer.

The driver and passenger looked at each other and shrugged. Very strange people here, they agreed. The passenger didn't raise the camera she had sitting on her lap. They drove on.

Doyle crossed the One as a familiar yellow Volkswagen drove up to the pumps, from the south.

"Hey Doyle," Sam the newspaper man greeted him. He held out ten bound copies of the morning's *Santa Rosa Dispatch*.

"Hey Sam." Doyle took the copies; they both ignored the crawling gawking vehicles on the One.

"So Doyle, you all are on the front page again, but I guess you knew that."

"Yeah, we figured. I don't know if I want to read it."

"Don't blame you. So how's Mrs. Satori doing? Terrible thing to go through."

"She's being looked after." Doyle looked south. "Did the cops wave you through?"

"Yeah, I felt like the Pony Express passing those fools waiting in line to gawk."

"Got time to chat?" Doyle asked. "I was just going to put some coffee on. We'll sit inside so they can't snap our picture and sell it to the *Dispatch*."

"Naw, gotta git, all this traffic is messing me

up. Maybe tomorrow if the traffic isn't so bad... as bad as your coffee, I mean."

Doyle chuckled. "All right, next time."

"See ya Doyle," and Sam drove on.

Doyle sat down on the stacked cases and opened one of the papers. He ignored the sensational front page ("ANOTHER MURDER IN LA SANGRE!") and turned directly to the classified ads.

It jumped out at him.

> **AUTO MECHANIC NEEDED**. 5 yrs experience in tuneups and brake repair. Apply in person. Emerald Ford, Santa Rosa Ave.

Across the One from where the realtor was waiting for her, Theresa saw the tall, thin yet rather attractive man in a down-home way, wearing coveralls, sitting on a short stack of boxes, reading the newspaper, and she recognized him as the man she'd just seen in the vision a few seconds ago, sitting on the church steps. He was 50 years old, she knew, and yet it was irrelevant. She pulled into the La Sangre Last Chance Gas Station.

Doyle looked up from the newspaper, got up and walked over to her car. The driver window was down. "I'm sorry ma'am, we're..." He couldn't speak.

"Closed," she finished his sentence. While he was the same man sitting on the church steps, he was far different now. Confident, bordering on cocky, which was fine, most men are that way. And this man certainly had a right to be cocky. Her Vision sharpened. This man, Doyle is his name, had just arrived at a deep, rich well after a lifelong walk through the desert. The perfectly round well was built of spherical river rocks, with a clean white-washed wooden bucket hanging from the hook and pulley, the handle of a wooden ladle peeking over the rim of the bucket.

"I mean," Theresa caught herself, "the deputy told me the gas station was closed, Doyle."

Doyle was lost in her eyes. "How...do you know my name?"

"Oh, uh...it's...it's on your coveralls." That was a good save; Theresa hadn't noticed his name patch. She already knew his name, felt his spirit, and fell in love with him, the first time she ever felt this way about a man. Why or how didn't matter. At 29 years old, she didn't question it. (Except that it's about damn time!)

Doyle looked down at his name patch that Lillian had sewn onto his coveralls for him; it seemed a lifetime ago.

"Eleven years ago," Theresa couldn't stop herself.

"Eleven years," Doyle looked at her. "I...I think I recognize you."

"I've seen you too, on the Old Redwood Highway. I'm Theresa, also known as Madame

Athena." It was the second time today, or ever, she divulged her dual identity.

"Madame Athena, Spiritual Readings," Doyle said. He was crestfallen, and his face showed it. He could see Madame Athena's house from the parking lot of the Adult Book Store, and he drove by it in both directions. That meant she probably had seen him from her driveway.

"It doesn't matter, Doyle," Theresa told him, wondering if anyone ever knew what beautiful blue eyes he had. A blue-eyed Italian. She knew that all of his life, nobody had ever really looked into his eyes.

"It doesn't matter," Doyle acknowledged what she said. He shook his head in wonder, "Nothing matters, does it?"

She continued to look into his eyes. "Good Lord," she declared softly, and extended her left hand out the driver's window.

Doyle took hold of it. He realized just how thirsty he was. He drank from her well.

EIGHT

MEMO

DATE: June 17, 1985
FROM: Sheriff Frank Daley, Sonoma County Sheriff Dept
TO: Martin Galiendo, State Attorney General's Office, Sacramento

Mr. Galiendo,

I'm not prepared to submit my final report regarding Ruby Rogers of La Sangre, CA. Beyond her placing the 911 call to report what became the murder of Sal Satori, she's saying nothing more, and I believe she knows more. I'm especially suspicious that she changed her hair coloring and general appearance right after the murder.

She's not a suspect for the actual crime, of course, but she's certainly a person of interest. I would appreciate your sending an agent to her for more questioning. Make it a female, Miss Rogers is a real pistol.

Thanks.
Frank Daley

Ruby had a neighbor drive her to the Santa Rosa Greyhound Bus Station ("Oh, I have to visit my sick niece!") where she took the four-hour ride north on US 101 to Eureka, CA, on the coast. As they approached Eureka at 1 PM, Ruby scanned the hillside east of the 101, and yes, there it was, St. Francis Abbey! It was beautiful, with a tower above the treeline, surrounded by green hills, just like Sleeping Beauty's Castle!

Excited, she unboarded and took her modest suitcase into the bus station, where she asked an attendant about transportation to St. Francis Abbey.

The weary old man studied Ruby—a fat, gray-haired plain-Jane, a little too old to become a nun—and looked out the window. "You could be in luck ma'am," he drawled. "See that station wagon out there, parked across the street?"

Ruby looked out the window. "Yes?"

"That's the convent's wagon. A couple of the Sisters must be in town, shopping. They should be able to give you a ride up there."

Ruby exhaled, relieved. She didn't know what to expect when she got here. She hadn't called the convent, not sure if they even have telephones, but it was like God was waiting for her outside, in a white, beat up old station wagon. Why wasn't there a door sign that read "St. Francis Abbey?" Don't they want people to know who they are?

Ruby thanked the man, went outside and crossed the street, just when two nuns exited a fabric store, carrying packages. This was all happening so perfectly!

"Hello Sisters!" Ruby said brightly as she approached them. "I wonder...would you be able to give me a ride to the abbey?"

One of the nuns was young, the other older. They nodded and smiled sweetly at her. The younger one opened the wagon's rear gate and deposited their packages.

"Do you have an appointment to see someone there?" the older nun asked.

"Well," Ruby responded, telling herself to keep her demeanor soft and demure, like a nun would. She was glad she no longer had her henna-red hair and that she had toned down her clothes, wearing a mid-calf black dress, black tights, and black lightweight coat. "I'd like to speak to someone, the Mother Superior I guess, about becoming a nun. I'd like to take my vows."

The Sisters looked at each other.

After a timeless moment, Doyle and Theresa unclasped their hands. She gave him a nod that clearly meant "We'll do this again," put her car into gear, and drove across the One and parked next to Nancy the Realtor's car.

"What was *that* all about?" Nancy asked Theresa as she got out.

"What was *what* all about?" Theresa decided she did not like Nancy at all, although she certainly knew her job. Theresa just wanted to get this transaction over with as quickly as possible.

"You and that...why, he's known up and down the coast as that crazy La Sangre Last Chance Gas Station man."

"Oh, I'm sure of that, Miss Hot-Shot Realtor. He's a fine man, a good man. Now why don't you just do your job and show me the house."

Properly chastised, Nancy led Theresa down the road and to the house in question. As quickly as Theresa had connected with Doyle, so she did with the weathered, wood-shingled house. Inside, the cozy living room had a rock fireplace with a wood stove insert and an ocean view; the kitchen and bath were both updated, and the two small bedrooms were adequate. Dual-pane windows throughout, and Nancy advised her that the house was rewired and replumbed within the last ten years. Yes, the house was meant for Theresa.

But do you really want to do this, Theresa?

Nancy saw Theresa's sudden doubt. "It needs to be re-carpeted and the interior painted," Nancy said, "but I can get some guys over here to..."

"No, it's not that. The house is fine, perfect in fact. The view of the ocean...."

"I think it'll help you when you do readings,

with the sound of the waves..."

"No!" Theresa interrupted her. "I mean yes, I'm going to live here, but no, not work here."

"So you're keeping your Santa Rosa house?"

"Yes, for work."

Well, there goes great listing opportunity, Nancy silently snarled. That stretch of Old Redwood Highway had been rezoned as strictly commercial, as Santa Rosa businesses creeped northward, and Nancy could have made a bundle on its sale. But she waited, watching Theresa, who was uncharacteristically uncertain, not quite solid on her feet; totally different from the solid, confident, even scary Madame Athena. This was more than Buyer's Doubt; maybe La Sangre frightened Theresa more than she let on. In any case, it was time to close the deal, before it was too late.

"A five hundred dollar check will hold the house for you," Nancy used her crisp, professional tone. "But you may lose the deposit if we don't proceed quickly. The Sellers are in the power position in La Sangre."

Theresa opened her purse. God, you'd better stop me from writing this check if I'm doing the wrong thing.

Ruby waited on the stone patio of St. Francis Abbey as she was told by one of the nuns. The view was spectacular, Eureka sitting like a jewel against the Pacific. This was even better than La Sangre, she thought, a more holy place where she would become a nun and serve God and help others. This was certainly where God wanted her to be. She would pay for her sin here, at St. Francis Abbey.

The Mother Abbess came out of the double doors onto the patio, accompanied by a postulate. Ruby stood up, ready to genuflect.

"Please, please, sit down, my dear," the Mother smiled at her and sat next to her on the stone bench. The postulate put a cotton quilt around the Mother's shoulders, who pulled it close. "It's rather cool out here, don't you think? Are you warm enough?"

Ruby nodded, she hadn't noticed, entranced as she was by the serenity around her, and now by this lovely, godly woman, from whom wisdom and patience emanated. The Mother nodded dismissal at the postulate, who silently nodded and left.

"What can I do for you, Ruby?"

"Oh Mother Superior, I want so much to...I...I just want to serve God, here at the convent, I want to take my vows and serve God."

The Mother smiled warmly. "I'm sure you do, my child. That is what we all must do, both within and outside the Abbey, to serve God." She looked towards the town below them, and the ocean beyond. "You told the Sisters that you arrived on a bus, is that right?"

Ruby nodded, wondering at the question. Was taking a bus the wrong thing to do? She would have thought it was more humbling than driving a car, which of course she didn't own.

"Ruby," Mother said gently, "the bus driver, the mechanics that keep the buses running safely, the baggage people, the ticket people, they are all serving God, each in their own humble way. Do you not think you can serve God in your current situation?"

Ruby was stumped. Her current situation? What was that? Just what was she doing in La Sangre all these years, besides setting herself up as the fat, henna-rinsed laughing stock? Worse, she sold poor Jessie Malana's tragic secret to Nathan, the newspaper man, she collected money from Jessie's sister, Maria, to spy for her in La Sangre and report anything she could discover, particularly about the psychiatrist, Dr. Owen, whom Maria suspected had caused Jessie to commit suicide. Did this mean Ruby was complicit in the attempted murder of Dr. Owen, and the resultant murder of Pastor Sal? Did she break the Fifth Commandment? Tears began, from the heart, not the false, showy tears Ruby had used at the Sunday service after Pastor Sal's death, just yesterday. She lowered her head, truly ashamed.

"Mother, I've never felt like this before," she

choked on her tears. "I don't know what to do."

The Mother waited a few moments before placing her experienced, gentle hand on Ruby's head. "My child, you're in pain. It seems you're running away from something, and you've come here to talk to me about it. Can you tell me what it is you're running away from?"

Ruby shook her head. "I'm so ashamed," she cried.

"Ruby, is there a sin you need to confess?"

"I don't know, I don't know if it was a sin. I'm so confused."

Mother waited until Ruby could look back up at her. This type of behavior from hopeful, naive women was quite usual in her job. "Ruby," she asked her, "did you see the movie, 'The Sound Of Music?'"

Ruby nodded, reaching for a handkerchief in her purse, surprised at the question. It was all she thought about on the bus ride up here. She fancied herself Julie Andrews as Maria,, who abruptly left the von Trapp Family and took the bus back to the Abbey, determined to take her vows.

"Do you remember, Ruby, what the Mother Superior told Maria when she returned to the Abbey?"

Ruby nodded, drying her eyes. "She sang 'Climb Ev/ry Mountain.'"

Mother smiled. "Well yes, the song says it all. But the Mother Superior also told Maria that she must find out what God's will is for her, as far as the Captain and his children were concerned. She told Maria that doing God's will was not just confined to the walls of the Abbey. What did she tell Maria she must do?"

"She...she told Maria she had to go back, to find out, to face her problems."

Mother nodded. "Now you apparently have a sin to confess, but besides confessing it to God, we must confess our sins to each other. It strengthens us, and provides support for each other. Now tell me, are you in any danger from anyone by going back and confessing your sin?"

"No," Ruby shook her head. "I don't think so."

"Have you done anything illegal?"

Ruby looked up at her. "Oh Mother, I don't know. I'm just so afraid."

Mother nodded and gave an understanding smile. "Yes, it's difficult to realize and confess our sins. But it's also humbling, and we must be able to humble ourselves before we can truly serve God. Now Ruby, suppose you went back, went to the proper party, and confessed your sin? And after that, if you like, and if you are able to, you can always come back here and you and I can talk some more. How does that sound?"

Ruby looked around her. "I thought..."

Mother sighed gently. "You thought you could hide here, where you'd feel sale? I understand, but that's something else we can talk about after you do what you have to do." She looked out at the Pacific. "You know Ruby, we sometimes show that movie, 'The Sound Of Music,' here in the Abbey."

Ruby looked at her, surprised. "You watch movies here?"

"Sometimes. Some of the sisters like to take field trips, go to the beach for a picnic, to San Francisco, go to a Giants game, to Great America and Santa Cruz."

"Oh," Ruby exclaimed, "it all sounds so wonderful!"

Mother gave her a meaningful look.

"But, yes Mother, I'll go back."

"I'll be praying for you here, my child. We'll all be praying for you."

One of the Sisters drove Ruby back down the hill to the Greyhound Bus Station, and left her with more promises of prayer. Ruby watched her drive off, standing on the sidewalk with her suitcase, not wanting to go into the depressing bus station to purchase a return ticket. Still, the better part of her felt light, energized, so she decided to put her suitcase in a locker and take the short walk down to the Eureka Wharf, which she saw from the Abbey. The ocean air was always cleansing for her; it's amazing that she took it for granted all those years in La Sangre. Were those wasted years? She didn't think so, she did plenty of church work. And yes, she also did plenty of mischief that she now had to atone for.

But you know what? Now that she thought about it, she doesn't have to tell the police anything. God has forgiven her, she'll just forgive herself. As far as those that died in La Sangre, well, it was God's will, wasn't it? She wasn't responsible. In fact, she was the one who called 9-1-1 to prevent the last one from happening.

Ruby realized her visit here, her talk with the Mother Abbess, had given her a chance to start anew. She could sell her home and move up here to Eureka. That could be God's will, because even if she doesn't take the vows, she could at least work at the Abbey, for nothing of course, just to be of service to Him. She won't need money, her La Sangre house will provide enough of that, she's already had offers shouted to her from the drive-by realtors. So she'll sell her house, rent a small home here, and what money she doesn't need she'll give to the church. Yes, she'll move to Eureka! That would be a good plan, that would be God's will.

But for now, she'll put her suitcase in a locker and take that walk to the Eureka Wharf.

"Excuse me! Do you live here, in Eureka?"

Ruby was so engrossed in her thoughts, still standing by the curb, that she hadn't noticed the shiny, blue Chevy Impala convertible pull up next to her.

"Do I...live here?" Ruby was surprised. *Do* I? Already? My goodness, God not only works in mysterious ways, He does so very quickly.

"Oh I'm sorry," the driver said. She was a young attractive woman in simple clothing: baseball cap, plaid shirt, and jeans. "I feel like a lost lamb. I just dropped a friend off here and she took the road map with her. I wonder if you could help me."

"Oh. Oh yes! Yes I *do* live here! I mean, I'm moving here, very soon."

"Oh good! Well maybe you can tell me. I'm heading south to Santa Rosa. Do you know how much longer it would take to use the coast route, Highway One, instead of staying on the 101? The One splits off from the 101 at Leggett, 90 miles from here and follows the coast, I know that much."

"Oh, well, the Coast Route takes longer, but it's a beautiful drive."

"Gee, I'd like to do that." The woman crinkled her nose. "But I don't know, going down the coast alone, it kind of scares me, being alone I mean. I'm from Portland, my sister just moved from there to Santa Rosa, and this is my first time coming down to visit her. I drove the 101 down this far, and dropped my friend from Portland off, but now I don't know if I should take the One or just stay on the 101."

"The One is really curvy, you just have to drive it slow, but it's really beautiful, and a lot of fun."

The woman lifted her Ray-Ban sunglasses over her forehead. "Where do you live?"

Ruby had already changed her programmed response to that question, as so many other La Sangre residents had. "I live in Santa Rosa."

The woman raised her eyebrows with an idea. "Say, if we're both going to Santa Rosa, would you like to ride along? You don't want to take that dirty old bus, do you?" She made a face at the bus station. "Besides, I'd feel safer driving along the coast with someone else along."

"I...I can't share in the driving. I don't drive."

"Oh that's okay! I'll do all the driving!"

God answers prayers! Ruby was certain that her visit to the Abbey and talking to Mother Superior had put her back on God's path. Everything seemed to be working out perfectly. This young woman was friendly enough, Ruby was sure it was safe. "Well..." she hesitated.

"Oh come on, it'll be fun! We'll talk and chat, I'll even buy you lunch. We'll have fun. By the way, my name's Bonnie. You know, like Bonnie and Clyde!"

"Now, we're not going to rob any banks, are we Bonnie?" Ruby was already feeling the gaiety.

"Well, maybe, if we run out of money!"

Bonnie teased. "Oh I'm just being silly! What's *your* name?"

"I'm Ruby!"

"Well, then we'll be Bonnie and Ruby! Hop in Ruby! But first, I'm going to run inside and call my sister, to tell her I'll be arriving later this evening instead of this afternoon." She opened her mouth in awe. "You know Ruby, we'll be able to watch the sunset while we're on Highway One! Won't that be wonderful?" She dashed inside the bus station, leaving the car running curbside.

She left her engine running? Ruby realized. What a trusting soul! She felt very safe.

Inside, Bonnie didn't insert a coin, she just dialed the number.

"Identify."

"California State Agent Bonnie Triplett, for Martin Galiendo."

"Passcode."

"537926."

"Pass*word*."

"Cyclone."

"Go ahead and leave your message."

"Hi Marty. I'm with subject Ruby Rogers now, driving her south on US 101 from Eureka, California to Leggett, then southbound on California Highway One to La Sangre. Subject appears pliant, I expect to receive information with little or no coercion. Will call when we arrive in La Sangre, ETA 1900 PDT."

NINE

After seeing the Help Wanted ad for Emerald Ford, and then reluctantly releasing his hand from Theresa, Doyle bound up the stairs to his room to change. He hesitated at first, thinking that maybe his coveralls with his name emblem on the front and "La Sangre Last Chance Gas Station" on the back would be a good walking resume of a working mechanic. Then he realized that after the long-held general belief of La Sangre being populated by "Those religious nuts," by this time it became more specifically "Those crazy Christians!" Doyle didn't want to deny what he was, but still, he'd better wear his civvies. When asked where he's been working as a mechanic, he'll just have to deal with it. Doyle put on his church clothes—his one white shirt and one red tie—and drove into Emerald Ford.

"So, you've been working in La Sangre, at the garage, for the past eleven years?" Dean Fiske, Emerald Ford's Service Manager, leaned back in his chair and studied Doyle. Dean was 50-ish, buzz-cut, clean-shaven, and wearing a spotless work shirt with an Emerald Ford name tag on the pocket, khaki's, and safety shoes.

As Doyle expected, he had no choice but to divulge his job experience, which was not inconsiderable. Now he wondered if he'd talked his way out of a job. But Dean smiled in a good-buddy manner. "So, you're getting the hell out of Dodge, right?"

Doyle shrugged. "Not sure yet, it all just happened, cops are patrolling the place, sad time for all of us. I live in a room above the gas station. I guess I'll find a place here in town. But I do know I don't want to work there anymore."

"I don't blame you," Dean said. "The family and I had dinner once at what you call the La Sangre *Saloon*? You know they didn't even have beer, and yet they call it a Saloon?"

Doyle nodded, waiting for Mr. Fiske to give him a yea or nay.

"Don't blame you," Dean repeated. "And Doyle, I really don't care about your religious beliefs, whatever they are, as long as you don't preach here."

Doyle nodded. "Of course."

"So, what do you know about electronic fuel injection?"

Doyle was ready for that one, he read *Road and Track* regularly. "Not too much. I know that Ford started using it two years ago." Well, he can kiss this job good-bye.

"We'll send you to classes for that," Dean shrugged. "Computers are becoming the new thing in automotive. Oh sure, I miss the old days of points and distributors, but we have to move on, don't we?"

Doyle nodded hopefully.

"We'll start you at seven bucks an hour."

Doyle's jaw dropped. That was twice minimum wage!

"You'll be scheduled Saturdays," Dean went on, "and work some Sundays if we need you for overload. You'll get paid shift differential for weekends, and time worked after 6 PM on weekdays."

Work some Sundays? Will he have to miss church?

Listen Doyle, there are a lot of guys that would kill for this job. I'm handing it to you, so don't blow it!

"You pay for your uniform," Dean was saying, "or we'll deduct it from your first paycheck if you like. You have safety shoes?"

"Yes."

"Well, keep them polished, your uniform clean. A lot of the guys have three or four uniforms, easier than going to the laundromat every day. We're all clean cut here, no beards, mustache okay, no hair past the collar line. Bring your own tools, you're responsible for them, not us. Lock your tool chest when you leave." He picked up the phone and dialed three digits. "Personnel will take your information, explain benefits, time off, all of that. We have a good medical and dental package...hi Gloria! We got our new mechanic, name's Doyle Seeno. S-E-E-N-O. I'm sending him over."

Doyle pulled into the La Sangre Gas Station just as Corey pulled the church van in front of the Grocery Store. Corey got out and went to the back of the van and Doyle walked over to him. A car coming from the south stopped next to them. The driver's window was down, a very unattractive couple stared at Doyle and Corey. "Hey!" the man called out. "Are you two related to that priest that got thrown off the cliff? Were you two his altar boys or something?"

"Move it!" Doyle yelled. "Before I have the cops arrest you disturbing the peace!" The car moved on, but not before the passenger snapped her 110 Instamatic camera at Doyle.

"Thanks Doyle." Corey was impressed. "I wanted to yell something but didn't know what."

"Well, I got my picture taken. She can sell it to the *National Enquirer*, captioned "Anger and Fear In La Sangre!" He looked inside the van. "Need a hand?"

"Not really, thanks. Just got a box of some perishables, there's already plenty of canned goods in the store. People are so busy moving they're not buying anything here. I just got these in case they're needed, besides a little shopping for my Mom. Pampers for the baby, a couple other things." He stared at Doyle. "Why am I telling you all this detail?"

Doyle chuckled. "Corey, none of us are at our best right now." He followed Corey into the store and watched him put the goods in the glass-front refrigerator. "How's she doing, your Mom?"

Corey shut the refrigerator door and turned to Doyle with a shrug. "Not so hot. At least she came out of the bedroom this afternoon, for the first time. Sat on the deck for a while, just looking at the ocean, holding the baby."

"Well, that's good I guess. Is Mrs. Freeman going to stay a while?"

"Yeah, I'd be lost without her. She's the only one who can get Mom to eat."

Doyle nodded and they went outside the store. As Corey locked the front door, Ralph and Matthew walked up.

"Morning guys," Matthew greeted them. "Mail in?"

"Yeah," Corey answered. "Let's go to the General Store."

"Say Doyle," Ralph said, "this is for you." He handed Doyle an envelope. 'Open it later, away from us. It's personal."

Doyle looked at him. "Bad news?"

"Not at all."

"Well," Doyle said to the others, "since all three of you are here, I just got some very good news."

He told them about his new job with Emerald Ford.

Up in his room, Doyle opened the envelope. Enclosed was a letter and a check.

> Monday, June 17, 1985
>
> Dear Doyle,
>
> I wanted to put this for writing, for the record. Just a month ago Sal made me the executor of his estate. He didn't want Connie to have to deal with it in the event of his death. I think Sal must have sensed the need to do this, in our talks he was certainly feeling his mortality, even young as he was. Maybe Sal knew something was going to happen, I don't know. He never mentioned anything like that to me.
>
> Among the things Sal mentioned in his estate was to give you the amount on this check. Normally this would be settled in the estate proceedings, but that can take some time, and based on our conversation this morning, you're ready to hop the next freight train out of town, as the saying goes. So I wrote this check on my

own account, which you can cash at any Bank of America. I'll be reimbursed out of the estate. I trust it will give you a jump start on your new life.

Remember that I'm always here for you. All you have to do is call.

Your friend,
Ralph Owen

The check was for $10,000.

As they entered La Sangre, Ruby returned to her sad loneliness. "Oh Bonnie, you don't have to leave right away, do you? I thought I'd cook us a nice dinner. We can watch the sun go down over the ocean."

Bonnie didn't respond, but pulled into the La Sangre Last Chance Gas Station.

"Oh, it's closed," Ruby told her. "The police closed it after Father's Day. Too many people would use it just so they could stare at us and take pictures."

"Oh no Honey," Bonnie responded. "I just need to use the pay phone to give my sister a new ETA."

"ETA?"

"Estimated time of arrival. And yes, I'd love to stay for dinner. In fact, I was hoping you'd say that!"

Ruby was overjoyed. "Oh now nice! And you can use my phone to call your sister."

Bonnie thought for a second. "Well, if you don't mind, Ruby, I'd rather call from here. My sister is, well, kind of funny, and if she starts an argument, which I'm sure she will, she always does, I'd rather you didn't have to listen to it."

"Oh, I understand! My sister is that way too!"

This was news to Bonnie. In all of Ruby's candor while driving down the One, starting with the fact that she lived in La Sangre, not Santa Rosa, she never mentioned a sister. Perhaps there was still more info Bonnie could gather.

"Tell you what," Ruby said, happy to have a friend; she hadn't had a close friend since Jessie. "Why don't you call your sister from here, and I'll walk down to the house and get dinner started. It's just down there, see the nice one, pink with green trim, at the end of the dirt road?"

"Oh, what a cute house! Okay Ruby, I'll see you in a few. Don't carry your suitcase down, I'll bring it along."

"Okay Bonnie! See you there!"

"Okay Ruby!"

Bonnie dialed the number on the pay phone, and after clearance, the FBI operator put Bonnie straight through to her contact, Agent Martin Galiendo.

"Hi Bonnie. I take it you're in La Sangre."

"Yes, hi Marty."

"How'd you do?"

"Well, you know I'm not a lawyer, but based on everything Ruby told me, she's definitely a conspirator to murder, however unwittingly. She didn't extort Jessie Malana, who volunteered information about her father's abuse, but Ruby sold that personal information to that so-called journalist, Nathan Steer. She also received money from Jessie's sister, Maria Malana, for 'keeping an eye on everyone in La Sangre,' particularly Sal Satori and Dr. Owen. Maria told Ruby she suspected Dr. Owen of having sex with Jessie while in therapy with him, and she had Ruby take a photo of Owen and give it to a private eye named Shawn, who passed it on to Maria, which Maria apparently gave to Bruno Logges, so he could identify and murder Owen."

Galiendo was quiet for a moment, digesting it all. "But Logges ended up killing Satori instead."

"Right. As we know, Satori pushed Owen out of the way and got shoved off the cliff himself. Ruby said she witnessed this from her home, close to the cliff."

"It sounds like you got it all."

"Well Marty, I'm going to Ruby's now to have dinner with her. Maybe I'll get something else, I don't know, but I don't want to push it."

"Right. You already got enough to bring her in for questioning at least, if not an arrest. So tell me, is Ruby Rogers one of those—what do they call them—La Sangre Christians?"

"Oh is she ever. She even wants to become a nun to 'atone for her sins.'"

"Oh brother."

"I know, a real fruitcake she is, but cute and funny in her way. She made the drive entertaining."

"Are you planning on spending the night at her place?"

"I think she's going to offer, but entertaining as she is, I'm not a glutton for lunacy. I'll stay at the Flamingo Hotel in Santa Rosa, unless you think I ought to stay with her. But I don't think she's a flight risk."

"Sorry Bonnie, but I think she is. She already tried to run away to the Convent in Eureka."

"Oh yeah, you're right. She told me she went there to become a nun."

"Well, she might try something crazy like that again, we'd better not take any chances." He sighed. "Yeah, you'd better stay with her. I hope she has a comfortable couch for you."

TUESDAY, JUNE 18, 1985

TEN

Ruby studied herself in the large mirror on the wall, the first time she really looked at herself since she got rid of the red hair, heavy makeup, push-up bra, and slutty clothes. After Madge worked her magic and made her plain, Ruby would at most do a cursory look at herself in the bathroom mirror, just enough to make sure her hair—she could hardly call it a "do" anymore—wasn't unkempt after a night in bed or from the ocean wind. But this horizontal wall mirror now facing her, about 6 feet by 4 feet, forced the issue.

And just who was that in the mirror, she wondered. Mirrors don't lie, but was that someone *new* in there, or was this how she always was? Did others see her this way, looking past her pathetic attempts to look young and alluring? Did they see what she now admitted to herself was a sham? Had La Sangre been laughing at her all these years, like they laughed at Doyle?

Doyle. Over the last few months she continued to make cruel remarks about Doyle, but the laughter wasn't returned any more; people would frown and not respond. Why did they stop making fun of him? Did Doyle have something to do with the murders? Was Doyle more sick than she thought? Was Maria Malana also paying Doyle to spy for her? And maybe, right now, Doyle is in the next interrogation room, waiting, checking himself out in the mirror...as if that would do any good.

But why in the world would a police interrogation room contain a mirror? Perhaps to give the visitors the opportunity to straighten themselves, make a good impression. She touched and patted her hair, straightened the collar of the white shirt inside her black sweater, and considered it nice of the police to provide this. She gave herself a smile, certain that after she told her story, like she told it to Bonnie, they would release her. This would be the confession of her sin that the Mother Superior suggested she do. It could cleanse her, God would forgive her, she could forgive herself, and then she could pursue selling her home to the highest bidder and going up to St. Francis Abbey in Eureka.

Hmph! Ruby felt her confidence returning. After the deputies brought her here so inconveniently, they'd better give her a ride home. As for that two-timing Bonnie Bitch...

"So what do you think?" Martin Galiendo

asked Bonnie Triplett as they studied Ruby Rogers through the glass.

"I think she's delusional. I got that from our ride down the coast. Oh, she believes she was morally wrong to sell Jessie Malana's personal information to a newsman, and to operate as a paid spy for Maria Malana. But I don't believe she knew that spying for Maria might have fueled Maria's rage; that she could have been the match to light Maria's emotional time bomb." She paused. "So Marty, even if Ruby didn't *know* her spying would lead to murder, would that still make her an accomplice?"

"It could, if only we had the letters that Ruby and Maria said they exchanged and then burned. That they burned their letters proves they were guilty of something, but without the actual letters, we have no proof. We found nothing in Maria's home, and as soon as the investigator calls us from Ruby's home, I don't expect he'll have found anything there either."

Bonnie sighed. She liked her work, but dealing with people who are out of touch with reality, people who are just harmless fools, saddened her. She was sad for Ruby, she didn't know how she felt about Maria Malana: that woman was a living Iron Maiden. But if Bonnie herself had gone through that poor woman's life, could she also have become a murderer? What made Bonnie any better than Maria, or Ruby? Bonnie was duplicitous herself, though it was her job. She cleared her throat.

"Marty, I know it's not within our scope of the investigation, but is the California State Attorney going to consider if, one, the crazy people in that town made it a hotbed of sickness, or two, if the town itself somehow causes people to go on tilt? 'It's an 'evil town, always was,' a lot of people say."

"What you're asking is what came first, the chicken or the egg. I can say one thing, if it's the latter, if that area is a vortex of evil, this will be the first California State investigation of psychic phenomena, at least that I know of."

"But Marty, I did feel that so-called vortex of joy and peace when I went to Hawaii, it truly feels like a paradise, I don't think I projected it."

"So what you're saying is, if there can be places of inherent goodness, why can't there be places of inherent evil? It sounds like one of those horror movies."

They exchanged raised eyebrows and then watched as Ruby gave herself a couple of futile primps in the mirror.

"Well," Martin sighed, "let's go in and do this, partner."

Matthew had to sleep on it before he responded to the letter Corey handed to him yesterday. He didn't even tell Lillian. She'd just left for her day shift at the hospital, Codding Kids Town wouldn't be open until noon, so, alone, he re-read the letter:

June 12, 1985

Mr. Matthew Grant
c/o Codding Kids Town
733 Codding Town Center
Santa Rosa, CA 95401

Dear Mr. Grant,

This is regarding your brother, Henry Grant. First off, he is all right, but for the past year he's been indigent here in Topeka, and squatting on city property. He has not responded to our warnings of possible incarceration.

You being his only living relative, I request you please call me as soon as possible to discuss the problem.

Thank you,
Donald Ellerbe
Detective Division
Topeka Police Department
Topeka, Kansas 66614

"Detective Division, Ellerbe speaking," the gruff voice answered.

"Hello, Detective Ellerbe. This is Matthew Grant. You sent me a letter about my brother, Henry."

"Oh yes," Ellerbe changed his sitting position for a probable long phone call. "Yes, Mr. Grant, I'm glad you called me back."

"I'm surprised you got hold of me. Except for the past year, I've been on the road all my life."

"So you've had no contact with your brother?"

Matthew froze, and couldn't use his full voice to admit "No."

Ellerbe was respectfully silent for a moment. "Well, that's what one of your old neighbors told me, the lady who lives across the street from your old home."

"Mrs. Schaefer? I'm surprised she's still alive."

"She is, very much so, though widowed. She told me the same thing that's on the 1946 police report, that you left home at 16 of your own volition, your mother let you go, and you stayed on the road as a carny..."

Matthew ignored the unintentional slur. Showmen were trying to get rid of that term, like other minorities were shirking their old slang references.

"...so someone at Carousel Park here suggested I try the Showman's League of America. They found you listed as a ride owner/operator, and directed me to Codding Kids Town."

"You're a good dick." Oops, were detectives also trying to shirk that outdated term?

"No I'm not," Ellerbe responded easily. "I wish I was still a cop. I miss my beat. Anyway, about your brother..."

Matthew steeled himself for the worse.

"Now, as I said in my letter, he's all right, but have you been in touch with him?"

"No." The last time he *could* have seen Henry was when he did a show in Topeka several years ago, and he didn't even take the time to call Henry, let alone stop by the house. Doyle was worried that his little brother would come looking for him at the carnival. Then again, Henry couldn't assume Matthew was working that particular show, and besides, he'd rather go to the movies than a carnival.

"Well, Mr. Grant, let me give you the rundown, I don't know how much of this you know."

"Nothing, since I left Topeka in '46."

"Okay. So after your mother died in '57, your brother continued to live in her house. It was paid off; your father used his G.I. Bill to take care of that, good of him to do so. Now, your mother made Henry the sole owner of the house..." Ellerbe paused.

"That's all right Detective, he earned it."

"Well, besides the few bucks Henry made managing The Grand Theater, he needed money to keep the theater going. He went through all the equity on his house and put it into the theater, which the owner was happy about but he never reimbursed Henry. They had no legal agreement between them, so there's nothing Henry can recoup. But then Henry became delinquent on his home property taxes and was so upside-down on his house that the bank repossessed it in 1970. After that Henry started living in The Grand."

Matthew's guilt, which he had so concealed, even from his wife, even from himself, began to rise like a monster. Henry has been living in a movie theater for sixteen years? How is that possible? "That old theater is still open?" Matthew asked instead.

"Not any more. It closed last year, the owner cut your brother some slack because he did appreciate how Henry kept the theater going, showing double-bills of those old movies that not many people came to see. Sometimes college kids, classic film buffs, but not many. By the way, Henry ran the projector himself, and he wasn't a member of the Projectionists Union, but they never bothered him. They may have understood the situation and just looked the other way, I don't know. I know the other Topeka theater owners sure did."

"So, the theater just went into the red?"

"Yep. Those old movies didn't even make him enough to support the place, let alone turn a profit. The only profit he made was that every Saturday at midnight he played 'The Rocky Horror Picture Show.' You ever see that?"

"No."

"Crazy movie. Well a lot of kids, college mostly, showed up in costumes and makeup, over and over at each showing. They'd make a mess of the theater, one time there was a fight, nothing serious. But your brother always kept things under control, and that's the only time he called us, was for that one fight. And after those midnight showings Henry would clean up the theater spic and span. When the kids got tired of seeing 'Rocky Horror,' Henry rented the theater out to live local bands. He paid for a cop, and the concerts were all pretty successful, no problems. Twice one of our local churches rented the theater for week-long revival meetings. Your brother thought that was pretty funny—he told me it was just like 'Elmer Gantry'—but at least he made a profit there, so he told me. I have to say Henry did his best. After that revival he canvassed all the other Full Gospel churches—we have a lot of them out here, as you know—for similar revival meetings, but he didn't get any more takers."

"So, he couldn't get anyone else into the theater?"

"No. He stopped renting films, the rock bands found other venues. You know, Mr.

Grant, things just change, people change, kids change, families change. Remember Boyle's Kiddieland?"

"Yeah." Did he ever. Boyle's Kiddieland was responsible for his life as a showman.

"They had to close down. That big new theme park, Worlds Of Fun in Kansas City, is only an hour away, offers a lot more for one price."

Matthew didn't want to be on this call, didn't want to hear any of this, didn't want to do this. "Detective," he asked, "back to my brother... well, did he have any friends?"

"None that I could see, none that anyone told me about. Mrs. Schaefer told me that while Henry was living alone across the street nobody ever came over. He just kept to himself, his TV, and The Grand Theater. But I can't call him a total loner. He'd stand outside the theater during the day, even after it was closed down, and try to talk to pedestrians about movies that he planned to show, but they always had to walk backwards away from him. Eventually they'd cross the street to avoid the 'Phantom of The Grand' they'd call him..." Ellerbe stopped. "I'm sorry Mr. Grant."

Matthew let out a breath. "That's okay Detective."

Matthew knew that his day of penance had arrived. Now he'll have to somehow deal with his little brother, who has spent his whole life in the old Grand Theater. It was all Henry knew. The Grand Theater and its movies. Henry certainly knew his movies, he lived in those movies. He was that way as a kid, and after their father's desertion...

And *your* desertion, Matthew.

"Anyway," Ellerbe cleared his throat, "despite Henry's efforts to find financiers to keep The Grand Theater as a landmark, even bring it back to its former glory, the old theater is going to be demolished in two weeks. No one cares, certainly not the public. The owner is dead but he gave theater to the city, he should have given it to your brother, at least he'd have the value of the property." Ellerbe paused for a breath. "So, we've let Henry stay there—there's a bed in the office, and Mrs. Schaefer bought him a portable shower and had it installed in the men's restroom..."

Kind of her to do that, Matthew thought. He'll have to call her.

"...but within two weeks he'll be out on the street, with no money other than his State Disability checks..."

"Disability? Physical disability?"

"No, it's for 'Mild to Moderate Mental Disorders,' they call it." Ellerbe cleared his throat again. "Mr. Grant, I'm afraid Henry's going to become part of the growing homeless population here in Topeka."

After they got married, Matthew had told Lillian about his little brother Henry, and they agreed they'd deal with whatever happened, whenever it happened. But Matthew never considered it could include his brother Henry dying alone, in the dead of winter, on the streets of Topeka, Kansas.

"I'm coming to get him," Matthew told the Detective resolutely. "As soon as I can."

"Well, you got two weeks," Detective Ellerbe responded. "Stay in touch with me, will you Mr. Steer?"

"Sure."

"Hello Ruby, I'm Arthur Valentine, a Public Defender for the State of California." He shook her hand. The poor thing had been crying; he pretended not to notice. "I'm glad you opted for counsel, after they read your Miranda rights."

"They talked me into it," Ruby reached for the box of tissues and cleaned her face. "But I told them two things: I don't have any money, and I want a Christian lawyer."

"That's why they called me," Valentine nodded. "I'm a Christian."

Ruby looked at Valentine warily. She was still upset from how Bonnie fooled her, being such a mean cop, especially after the friendly cheer of their drive down the coast. They'd chatted and laughed, like girlfriends; they stopped for lunch at a lovely seaside restaurant in Anchor Bay—Bonnie paid for it—and even took a few minutes to explore Fort Ross where, in the restored Russian Orthodox Church, Ruby knelt in a pew and asked God to please show His will to her. Was she really meant to become a nun? She herself wanted it, but did God want it? Ruby was especially touched when Bonnie knelt next to her and crossed herself. When they got back in the car to finish their trek to La Sangre, Ruby asked Bonnie if she was a Christian, and Bonnie smiled and said yes. That was when Ruby knew she could bare her soul to Bonnie, even more specifically than she did with the Mother Superior.

"*Are* you a Christian?" Ruby now doubtfully asked Attorney Valentine. "A lot of people say they are but they aren't. Don't lie to me, or you'll be using our Lord's name for your own vain reasons."

"Yes Ruby, I am a Christian, and as disciples of Christ we dedicate ourselves to the Truth, no matter how much it may hurt. Jesus never said it was easy. When I took the Oath of the American Bar Association, like the Hippocratic Oath that Doctors take, I pledged to God that my job would be to find the truth, apply the law, and trust the American Justice System to reach the proper verdict and sentencing."

Verdict and sentencing. Ruby stiffened up. She took a breath. "So, Mr. Valentine, Sir, am I actually being charged with something?"

"Yes Ruby, you are. You're being charged as an accessory to murder."

"NOOOOOO!" Ruby pressed her hands over her face. "PLEASE GOD NOOOOO!"

Mr. Valentine sat still and watched her, and empathized.

Once Ruby's passionate cry lowered to where she could talk, she asked "What about that woman? That Bonnie! She lied to me. She *lied* to me! We were praying together in church, and I felt that God had given me a friend. I asked her if she was a Christian and she said yes! What do they call that, when a policeman traps you?"

"Entrapment."

"Yes! Can't we sue them for entrapment?"

Valentine sighed and shook his head. "We could, Ruby, but that would only ensure a trial, and it could tear you apart, it can tear anyone apart. No, I think I can get you off without suing, but Agent Triplett's behavior is my trump card, and they know I'll use it if I have to. But now," he placed his hands on the table, palms up, "let's pray. And remember Ruby, 'In God there is no fear.'"

Ruby placed her hands in Valentine's, still a little uncertain, but she bravely took another chance.

After the prayer, Mr. Valentine said "Ruby, why don't we start from the beginning."

"The very beginning?" Ruby was wiping the tear remnants from her face. "You mean like when Jessie Malana first came to La Sangre? And I thought that at last I had a friend?"

Valentine nodded.

Elaine Schaefer answered the phone on the sixth ring. "Hello?"

"Hello, Mrs. Schaefer?"

"Yes?"

"This is Matthew Grant. Remember me, from across the street?"

Silence.

"Yes Matthew, I remember you," she finally responded. She wasn't hostile or rude, just cold. "Detective Ellerbe told me he was looking for you. Apparently he was successful. Funny, I was going to let this call go to the answering machine, but something told me to take it."

Matthew waited until he was certain she was through. She could have thrown the kitchen sink at him, but she didn't. "I'm calling about my brother, Henry."

"Henry, that you deserted forty years ago, and you call him your *brother*?"

Matthew had that coming. "I...I'm coming to get him."

Silence.

"Mrs. Schaefer, are you aware of his situation?"

"Matthew, how can I *not* be aware of his situation! And I must apologize for my coldness, but I can't say it's none of my business. Ever since you ran off when you were 16, leaving your younger brother alone with his deserted mother, I'm all he's had. I've known you boys since you were toddlers, babysat for you, you'd stay over here when necessary. I *am* involved Matthew, Henry Grant *is* my business. Now, I can't very well take him in here at my age..."

"Of course not. I wouldn't expect you to."

She gave a resigned sigh, and softened her tone. "I'm sorry, Matthew, I'm probably judging you, I'm sorry." She gave herself a moment's break. "When the neighbors and people talk about Henry Grant and how he lives in his fantasy world of movies, I ask them to go through desertion of his father and older brother, taking care of a mother who lost her mind over it and died before her time, and then see how well they walk on this Earth."

THURSDAY, JUNE 20, 1985

ELEVEN

Anne Owen changed the title of her manuscript, *The Mystery Of La Sangre* since, as Ralph commented, it sounded too much like a romance novel with the cover of a beautiful busty girl in a flimsy negligee feigning resistance to an amorous shirtless ranch hand. Besides, Anne was certain that during Sal's funeral, she'd overheard Nathan Steer whispering to his wife, "This will be a great chapter in *The Secret Of La Sangre*!" How *dare* he steal her title! But it was a godsend because her new title was much better: *Murder By The Sea: The True Story Of La Sangre*.

After the funeral let out, Ralph told Anne that he had to run into Santa Rosa for some meds. She assumed they were for Connie Satori, who seemed beyond grief and almost catatonic, a dramatic point Anne just added to her manuscript.

Pastor Satori's widow, Connie Satori,
wearing a tasteful black suit, a modest black hat

> with a veil, and low-heeled black shoes, sat in the front pew, holding her infant son Freeman, and surrounded by Grace Freeman and Corey. Behind them sat friends Matthew and Lillian, and Julie and Nathan.
>
> Dr. Owen, accompanied by his wife, sat across the aisle from Connie, keeping watch over her. She seemed to have become his unofficial regular patient, such was her catatonic state. Indeed it wasn't grief she displayed, more of a zombie-like appearance.
>
> As would be expected, the rest of the town engaged in a "Who can cry the loudest?" contest. Apparently the louder you cry, the holier you are. Amazingly, the interim pastor, William Farrow, kept some kind of order throughout the whole bizarre affair.

Maybe, Anne thought, she would end the book with this, the funeral scene, unless more things continued to happen in this ridiculous town. Her book was really writing itself, and perhaps it was now finished. Anyway it was time for her to contact the several Yellow Book listings of San Francisco writer's agents she'd found in the Santa Rosa Public Library. With Ralph out of the house for a few hours, she made the first call, the one that had the biggest Yellow Book ad.

"San Francisco Literary Agency, Cindy

speaking, how may I help you?"

"Hello, my name is Anne Owen," she had practiced her speech. "I live in La Sangre..."

Cindy Carlton snapped to attention, catching the attention of a co-worker. "You live in La Sangre?" The co-worker quietly picked up her extension.

"Yes, my husband and I have lived here for ten years." Anne stopped, and tempered her nervousness. This was exciting, her first step. "Last year I wrote a book about everything that goes on here in La Sangre..."

Cindy and her co-worker exchanged looks.

"...and I titled it *Murder By The Sea: The True Story Of La Sangre...*"

Cindy and co-worker's expressions changed to silent laughter. They had just signed Nathan Steer for *The Secret Of La Sangre*, and they were within a day or two of getting a hardback contract.

"...and I wonder if you'd be interested in representing me."

"Well, thank you very much, Mrs. Owen," Cindy gave the same response she used eleven years ago when anyone from Berkeley who claimed they knew Patty Hearst had written their own books like *I Was Patty Hearst's Roommate* or *I Dated Patty Hearst*. "We actually have already signed an author for his book, and I'm afraid signing on someone else with a book on the same subject would be a conflict for us."

"Does that so-called 'author' happen to be Nathan Steer?" Anne blurted out. Oh shit. This is why she needed Ralph to help her. He had warned her to be professional, after firmly refusing to help her sell her manuscript. He read it and hated it, which led to some heated arguments that Anne was sure the neighbors could hear. But Ralph was firm. "It's your book, I won't support it, you find your own agent."

Cindy ignored Anne's outburst. "Miss Owen..."

"*Mrs.* Owen. I'm married to Ralph Owen, the psychiatrist here in La Sangre."

Cindy of course knew that name from Nathan's manuscript, which used quotes from Dr. Owen rather liberally and probably off the record. Well, that's the publisher's lawyers' problem. All Cindy cared about was that the San Francisco Literary Agency was going to get a hell of a commission on Nathan Steer's book.

"I'm sorry Mrs. Owen, we won't be able to read your manuscript, but there are other agencies here in San Francisco. Very good ones."

"Like who?"

"Well, I can't refer you to one, but you can look in the Yellow Pages under Literary Agencies...."

Anne's line clicked and left a dial tone.

Cindy shrugged. "So much for her," she said to her coworker.

"She sounded like a crackpot."

"Yeah," Cindy replaced the receiver. "Lizzie, the more we work on the Steer manuscript, the more I'm convinced that that town does have some strange power that makes people go..." She flailed her hand to grab hold of the appropriate word.

"Crazy?"

"I'd go for 'insane.'"

Other than what Connie wore and who was present, the section on Sal's funeral in Anne's book was foggy, because few people in La Sangre—and somehow, strangely, including Anne herself—would ever be able to actually *remember* it. The 35 minute funeral was a congregational blackout. They didn't know what to do with it or where to put it. And while everyone agreed that Pastor Farrow was a nice enough man, warming to him just wasn't possible.

It was like when John F. Kennedy was assassinated 22 years ago, nobody wanted to even look at Lyndon B. Johnson. He was big and ugly with an annoying drawl, looking incongruous while taking the Presidential Oath on Air Force One, standing next to John Kennedy's brave, beautiful widow in her blood-stained pink suit, which she refused to change. "No!" she righteously declared. "Let them see what they've done!"

La Sangre wanted Sal Satori back, especially the old-timers, most of whom were selling their homes through whatever realtor would take the lowest commission. While it's true the old-time religious were bothered by Pastor Sal's recent evolution to liberation, enlightenment and anti-legalism after the events of the last Father's Day, they couldn't deny their love for the man, who was always there for them, 24 hours a day.

Cops were still controlling traffic on The One, heavier today due to the funeral, which the news media had liberally announced. Doyle was able to get the morning off from his new job at Emerald Ford, and stood vigilant with a cop at the front door of the church. Only townspeople and those on a guest list of Sal's former Fresno church and the San Francisco District Office were allowed.

Ralph, Matthew, and Corey agreed that beginning the day after the funeral, they would reopen the La Sangre businesses: the Last Chance Gas Station, General Store, Grocery Store, Antique store, and the La Sangre Saloon. No one could venture down the road leading to the homes, and a deputy was assigned to that duty.

Matthew knew that Lillian could have taken time off from the hospital to ride with him to Topeka, but he had to do this himself. He just didn't know how to tell Lillian.

But Lillian beat him to it at dinner. "Matthew, you need to go get your brother, alone. Face him, and face yourself."

Matthew gave her a sheepish smile. She was the only woman in the world who could kick his ass, and he loved her for it.

"Yeah Lilly, I can do that. I already talked to Corey about bringing Henry back and putting him in the spare room above the garage."

"That's a good idea. But what would Doyle think of that? He'd have to share the bathroom with a stranger, after all these years, up there alone?"

Matthew put down his fork and wiped his mouth. "He told me he's thinking about moving into Santa Rosa, getting an apartment."

"Really? He has the money for that? First and last month's rent, all of that? He just started his job at the Ford dealer."

"He said he did."

Lillian was silent. "I'm surprised that it bothers me, Doyle moving on. After all these years I feel I'm finally getting to know him." She lay down her napkin. "Is Micah handling the gas station okay?"

"He seems to be."

Lillian wasn't sure how she felt. All this happening; Sal's death, Doyle leaving, now Matthew is going to Kansas, alone, to pick up his long lost brother. For the first time since she and Matthew married, she was worried. "Are you through?" she reached for his plate.

"Yeah. Thanks. And thanks for bringing it up, about my going to get Henry, alone."

"You would have brought it up. I just saved you the trouble."

Lillian was suddenly uncomfortable. What are we setting in motion?

JUNE 21-30, 1985

TWELVE

The visitation room at the Sacramento State Prison was what Corey expected: army green cinder block walls with matching concrete floor, making the room echo with the slightest movement. He sat on one of the gray plastic chairs lined against the wall, that faced ten partitioned booths on the opposite wall. The booths were lined with acoustical tile, with a plastic chair, a wall phone, and a plexiglas window.

Corey saw Maria before he was called forward. She was led by a small scary female guard from a door behind the booths. Even in her orange prison jumpsuit, no makeup, hair tied behind her, she was beautiful. She didn't see Corey, didn't even look across the waiting room. Corey wondered if they'd told Maria who her visitor was, or if they just yelled "Malana! You got a visitor!" The guard put Maria in the booth on the far left end and stood behind her.

Another female guard came up alongside Corey. "Mr. Freeman, booth #1." She pointed.

Corey kept his eyes on Maria as he

approached the booth, willing to break the ice first. But she stared straight ahead; if she saw him in her peripheral vision, she gave no sign. Corey sat down and picked up the phone, but she continued staring ahead, and he couldn't quite catch her eye.

Maria's facial expression could have been described as flat and affectless, but it may have been one of a hundred different emotions. Corey supplied for her the one he wanted: that she still had some feeling for him, that their two days together at her beach house were indeed wonderful, special, not simply a ploy. ("Well Corey," she had told him when she kicked him out of her beach house that last time, "you'll never have it that good again. Oh you'll search for it, but you'll never have it that good again.")

Yeah, how Corey has searched for it. He picked up his receiver but Maria just sat there.

"Pick up the phone, Malana!" the guard behind her snapped, loud enough for Corey to hear through the glass. Maria waited for as long as she thought she could get away with it, then picked up the receiver.

"Hi Maria," Corey said, trying not to sound too hopeful.

Her ambiguous expression remained.

"I was afraid you wouldn't want to see me," he attempted.

Her mild shrug was her first communicative

movement since she was ushered in.

"I mean," Corey was encouraged by her slight reception, "thank you for seeing me."

"We only have five minutes, Corey," she said bluntly, a fast step from passe into hostility. "After all, I'm a goddamned celebrity here, didn't you know? Haven't you seen the news? Everyone wants to talk to me. Barbara Walters wanted to see me, can you believe that? I told her to fuck off. Plus, every woman in this cell block doesn't want to just *talk* to me, they *want* me, period." She turned her head towards the guard and raised her voice, "And some of the guards too!"

The guard ignored her.

Corey exhaled and decided he'd better just get to business. "Maria, Dr. Owen..."

Her eyes widened at the name.

"No Maria, he wants to help you. He wants to be the psychiatrist for your defense! Your lawyer won't return his calls. So..." Corey was at a loss.

"So what?"

"Maria, he tried to help your sister, all those years in therapy with her. He told you at the cliff that night that it wasn't him who had sex with Jessie."

Her face actually softened. Her jaws unclenched, her lips decompressed, her eyes relaxed and finally met his.

"Did he say that? At the cliff? I was so..." she shook her head. "I was in what the prison psychiatrist calls my rage. 'My rage.' As if I need a fucking psychiatrist to tell me that!"

"Yes, at the cliff that night, Dr. Owen said that he didn't have sex with Jessie, and he's sure that Bruno heard him too, and believed him, but Bruno was so wound up...."

"Yeah, old Brutus had his own rage to deal with. His way of controlling it was by being a conceited gym rat, that poor sorry sonofa...."

"Anyway Maria, please, at least ask your lawyer to talk to Dr. Owen."

"So," Maria shrugged with no commitment, "if it wasn't Dr. Owen who had sex with Jessie, who did? You said you didn't, were you lying to me?"

"No, you knew I wasn't."

"Then who?"

Corey took a deep breath. "It was my father."

But for the plexiglas, Maria might have lunged at Corey. "YOUR FATHER THE PREACHER MAN? HE'S THE ONE WHO FUCKED MY JESSIE?"

"Voice and language down, Malana!" the guard warned her.

Maria smirked and lowered her voice. "Your father the preacher man," she said again. "I should have known. How stupid of me, and of Ruby, for that matter, not to know that."

Corey stopped. This was harder than he thought it would be. He was actually talking against own father, who had been murdered. Who was the victim here? Everyone? The world, Corey's world, wasn't just upside down, it was non-existent. Suddenly he wanted to be on the road again, the asphalt and white lines flashing past him. The road was his drug, and he needed it, now.

They were both quiet for what felt like a minute, though it probably wasn't. Time was at a premium on the prison phone line. Corey was relieved when Maria finally broke the silence, with a softer tone, and looking straight at him.

"Corey, I'm truly sorry that I used you like I did. I really did enjoy my time with you, and of course, I know you did." She smirked. Corey was encouraged with, at last, a sign of recollection, of their 48 hours of touching, needing each other, relishing and devouring each other.

"I hope," Maria continued, "that you can remember it as just a wild frolic on the beach, nothing more. Don't build your life on it, Corey. Jay told me..."

"Jay? You know him?" Corey hadn't thought about him since that night at the truck stop, when Jay pressed his finger against Corey's sternum and said "Get your ass home! And I don't mean Bakersfield!"

Maria avoided the question. "Just forgive

me, Corey, if you can, and move on with your life. Please, *please*, move on."

The phone went dead.

"Maria..."

She was still looking at him, her lips moving silently.

He would spend the rest of his life wondering what she said.

"Hi, I'm Corey, and I'm a sex addict."

"Hi Corey."

"I saw..." he looked around at the men, twelve of them tonight. "I saw Maria earlier today, for the first time since..." He couldn't remember.

Whoever is speaking during 12 Step has the floor for three minutes. No one else can interrupt or ask questions. But they all knew who Corey was, son of the murdered preacher, and they knew who Maria was, he'd been forthcoming about all of that. But all such personal data stayed in that room in the Santa Rosa National Guard Armory, a code of brotherhood that all the addicts shared and kept. They were battle-scarred and just trying to fly right, not too dissimilar from Vietnam Vets. Even after the meeting, when everyone gathered around to drink coffee and chat, personal information was only volunteered, never sought.

"It's Maria I'm hooked on," Corey continued, "or the two-day memory of her. Maybe I'm not addicted to sex, but to her, and it's our time together I keep trying to duplicate out there, with the lot lizards and the whore houses...and the brown wig I asked them to wear. But now she's in prison, locked up, so shouldn't that put an end to it? Shouldn't that force me to get on with my life, like she told me I should? I don't want to, but I'm going to the book store and watching porn every night. I am fucking sick of this bullshit!"

Corey sat with a crash back into the steel folding chair, ignoring the flash of pain...or perhaps loving it.

There was more silence than usual. It took almost two quiet minutes before another man stood up.

"Hi, I'm Randy, and I'm a sex addict."

"Hi Randy."

Afterward, as the men gathered around, drinking coffee and chatting, Gary—72, still fit, single-not-lonely, and the group leader of what he considered his boys—approached Corey and placed his hands firmly on his shoulders. "Hey Corey, are you sure you're not being too hard on yourself? You're only eighteen, we all went a little crazy back then, we were all young and dumb and only listened to our dicks. I think you're just coming down from that now. All right, you're going to those silly adult book stores, but I'm not so sure you're actually an addict."

Corey looked into Gary's lucid eyes. He liked Gary, and trusted him, he was smart and was good at decision-making; but it somehow bugged Corey that Gary always allowed for benefit of the doubt. When Gary listened to an individual after the meeting, he was kind, attentive, and if a guy went off the wagon, Gary would say, "I don't care, and neither does God, what you did last night. It doesn't matter. You're here now, so let's move forward."

But Gary wasn't Pete, nor Sal, and certainly not Jay. Corey wanted Gary to be more forceful, like when Jay thrust his finger into Corey's sternum and told him to "Get your ass home!" Gary was just too goddamned...understanding and forgiving, which Corey didn't want right now.

"So Gary, you think I'm being too hard on myself? So I'm not an addict, I'm just a kid with a permanent hardon? But if I'm not an addict, like you say, then what am I, just plain crazy? I found out last year that my father isn't my real father, that I was adopted; that same day I meet the man who *is* my real father, and then he gets run over by Jessie, after pushing me out of the way. Then a year later, last week, my adopted father gets murdered at the order of Jessie's sister, to whom I'm addicted? Oh but sure Gary, I'm okay, nothing wrong with me. I'm not really a sex addict, right? I'm just fucking insane! Is that it, Gary? Am I just fucking insane?"

Gary couldn't answer Corey's very legitimate question, at least not in the way Corey wanted to hear. Corey was simply asking "Where is God?" Responding with "God is everywhere!" would be inadequate, because "everywhere" doesn't include the depth of the human soul, which has free choice to open or shut its door.

When Corey came to his first meeting, shortly after his father Sal died, he was forthcoming about who he was and about his background. Gary thought then that Corey, being a Preacher's Kid, would have mastered the Christian tools available to him, to forgive and move forward. After all, the 12 Steps were just Jesus' words, secularized. But as Gary observed at the opening of each SAA meeting, poor Corey couldn't even get through the Serenity Prayer, freezing up on "God grant me the serenity to accept the things I cannot change."

But Corey wasn't through with his rather literate rant. "Yeah, sure Gary, I've been getting my licks in. But it could lead to addiction, right? You said yourself that nobody starts doing anything with the *intention* of becoming an addict, it just happens to us before we're even aware of it, right? So what are we all supposed to do: never drink, never touch drugs, no R-rated movies, no rock music or dancing, no novels with sex and profanity, and most importantly, don't have sex until we're married? Does that make life more 'correct?' I know people who did all that stuff and they're bored in their marriages, bored in their life. They just go to church and sit there, scared to death of that sinful world outside the church doors. Maybe they should have gone the way of the prodigal son and tried things so they can find out there's no lasting kick to them!"

Gary was still holding Corey's shoulders firm, and Corey reached up and grabbed Gary's arms. "So I'm angry and miserable, and I use sex as a release, but I'm not an addict? So tell me Gary, am I fucking insane? Is that it? Because you've said insanity is just doing the same thing over and over and expecting different results, right?" Corey moved in close, nose-to-nose with Gary. "SO TELL ME, MAN! AM I JUST FUCKING INSANE?"

Gary held Corey's gaze for what felt like a minute, then looked down. His batting average of seeing people finally meeting Jesus and receiving the ability to forgive—not to mention receiving the fearless, non-circumstantial Joy in their souls—was .025 at best.

Gary knew he'd never stop fighting, but he was also getting tired. He nodded in surrender, slapped Corey on the shoulder, and went over to the coffee table, where he had a conversation with Randy.

Julie waited for a couple days after Sal's funeral before she asked her husband, "Nathan, you had a tape recorder in your pocket during Sal's funeral, *and* at the Sunday service the morning after he died, didn't you?"

"Come on Jules, you know I did."

"But...how could you do that?"

"Wait a minute now babe, when we were first dating I told you my dream was to become a journalist, a real journalist who cracks a story, not some powder-puff writer for the local newspaper, which is what I am, and I can't live with it anymore. You knew that when we met; our first date, I told you that at an outdoor table at Ron's Burgers on Fourth Street in Santa Rosa, or don't you remember?"

Julie shook her head. "I remember that Nathan, I just thought you could turn it off when you had to."

"Did you expect that reporter to 'turn it off' in the kitchen of the Ambassador Hotel in Los Angeles when Robert Kennedy was shot? And the only footage we have of his brother John being assassinated in Dallas is from a family man who just happened to be shooting the Presidential caravan with his eight millimeter camera! Should that man have put his camera down, not shot it, out of respect? Julie, am I supposed to not take pictures, not take notes or recordings? Come on Jules, get on board with me here! I'm your husband." He put his hands on his wife's arms, squeezing lightly. "This is who I am. The man you married." He looked down. "I was going to take you out to dinner tonight and tell you this, but I'll tell you now." He looked back up. "San Francisco Writer's Agency got me a hardback contract with Viking Press! They'll have it in the bookstores by August 1, and they've already contacted Stu Waterman! Do you know who he is, Jules? He's the god of Hollywood! My book could become a major motion picture! Babe, please stay with me on this! We're on the highway to success, money, and fame! Please Julie, let's be happy, for the first time in our lives! Or at least let *me* be happy!"

Julie was shocked. She thought they were *already* happy!

Nathan misread his wife's sudden gushing tears as joyful agreement.

"Atta girl," he put his arms fully around her and brought her close.

Julie buried her head in his shoulder, wetting his plaid shirt. He didn't understand.

NEVADA US 50 EAST
THE LONELIEST
ROAD IN AMERICA
FALLON 62
ELY 320

Matthew had reached Carson City, Nevada, by 2 PM, just four hours after kissing Lillian good-bye in the hospital employee parking lot.

"It's slow in the ER today," Lillian had told him, "but I still only have five minutes."

"Just enough time for another good-bye kiss. Gonna miss you Lilly."

"Really?" she smiled mischievously. "'The Road' isn't going to tempt you to stay out there? I'm just one of the many women in the world who has The Road as her rival."

"Aw, I'm tired of the road, you know that. I don't want to go back out there. Now," he shrugged playfully, "I'm not saying I won't flirt with the waitresses...."

"Oh *that's* okay," she slapped his arm playfully. "Flirt away, but come home."

"Yeah, I will," Matthew exhaled, "with kid brother in tow."

She put her hands on his cheeks. "Matthew, we'll handle it together. Okay?"

Matthew hesitated. "Okay."

"And you watch your speedometer on those lonely stretches in that muscle car of yours."

"Now *that* I can't promise."

Indeed, once Carson City was in his rear view mirror, he stepped on it, relishing the deep roar, savoring the power of his orange 1970 Barracuda. But once he saw "US 50, The Loneliest Road In America," the unresolved, buried past emerged.

In 1936, when their father, Ulysses, first took them to Boyle's Kiddieland in Topeka, Kansas, Matthew was six and Henry was four. Matthew was astounded by all the mechanical gadgets, miniature helicopters he could actually fly, smiling whales he could ride the waves with, cars that circled, and everything went up and down, round and round. The kiddie Ferris Wheel took the happily screaming Matthew and Henry up to heaven and back down again, and back up, over and over. The Merry-Go-Round's horses were far prettier than the real horses of their neighbors, as they danced up and down, round and round, to a joyful calliope.

But Matthew's favorite by far was the kiddie roller coaster, that took them up, then plunged down, around a turn, up and down again twice more, another turn that sent them screeching into the station to a fast stop. The operator, a short ugly old man with a partial-teeth smile asked "Want to go again?" and all the kids gave a joyous scream. The second time around was even better than the first.

Henry liked Boyle's Kiddieland okay, and certainly joined in whenever Big Brother Matthew said "Daddy, can we go to Boyle's Kiddieland? We made our beds! I helped Henry." But Henry found his own childhood passion when he saw his first movie, "Snow White And The Seven Dwarfs" at Topeka's ornate Grand Theater in 1937. Although Henry loved the seven dwarfs, the Wicked Witch scared him, and Matthew tolerated Henry sleeping in his bed that night. Henry told him he was afraid that the witch might climb through their bedroom window and make him eat a poisoned apple. "Don't let her get me Matthew!" Henry pleaded. "Ah, she ain't gonna get you, go to sleep!" was Matthew's reply.

Two years later, in 1939, when Henry saw "The Wizard Of Oz" at The Grand, once again there was a Wicked Witch. Was there always a Wicked Witch in the movies? He slept in Matthew's bed again that night.

Ulysses Grant enlisted in the Marines right after Pearl Harbor was bombed on December 7, 1941. He kissed his wife and boys good-bye at the train station, and was gone. Although all of Ulysses' pay was sent to Daisy, she diligently got a job at Topeka's Woolworth store, and when the Topeka Army Base opened in late 1942, she transferred there. Mrs. Schaefer, whose husband went into the Army, lived across the street. She and her husband had no children of their own so she enjoyed watching the two very easy boys after school and accepted no pay for it.

In September 1945, one month after Hiroshima was destroyed, Daisy received a telegram from the United States Defense Department of Defense, stating that Ulysses Grant would be returning home from Japan. On that very day there was the highly anticipated knock on the Grants' front door, and Daisy and Matthew and Henry rushed to open it. Their father was standing there in full uniform, minus his right arm, with a Japanese woman, whom Henry thought was very pretty. "May we come in?" she asked in perfect English.

Dumbfounded, Daisy Grant and the two boys backed up from the door as Ulysses and the woman came in, saying nothing. Ulysses didn't hug or kiss his wife, he didn't touch the boys with his good left arm, he just kept his eyes on the Japanese woman as she took Ulysses by the left hand and led him to the small couch that only holds two. They sat on the couch, and Ulysses continued to just look at the woman.

"My name is Mia," the woman broke the silence, speaking mostly to Daisy. "I was born and raised in Japan. Ulysses met me in a..." she considered the two boys, "in a gentleman's parlor in Tokyo, where I worked since I was twelve. My parents told me to use the name Mia, not Miyoshi, learn English, speak it well and especially with no accent. I practiced my R's and L's. I learned all I could about America from my American customers. I carefully chose the best man to go to America with, and that is Ulysses.

He may not be not the most handsome man of those I have met, nor the richest, but I know he will be a good husband to me and I will be a good wife to him. If he asks me to work for him, I will. We are going to live in San Francisco, and he won't be seeing you again."

Daisy Grant's life would from that moment be divided as Before and After Hiroshima. The last lucid line she spoke for the rest of her foggy life was "I want my husband to tell me this."

Ulysses didn't look at his wife, only at Mia. "Mia speaks for me," he said.

Henry thought he finally saw the Wicked Witch in person, only she was pretty.

Matthew suddenly wanted to go, no *needed* to go, to the Kansas State Fair, which was opening in two days, and had all the bigger rides that Boyle's didn't. When his mother had told the boys the date of their father's return, Matthew was thrilled that it would be in time for Dad to take them to the State Fair.

Daisy Grant couldn't go to work, she stopped going to church, barely cooked and did little housework. The family doctor gave her some pills, which she took for the rest of her life, and which eventually killed her at age 46.

Two days after Ulysses' brief visit, Mrs. Schaefer took the despondent boys on the bus to opening day of the Kansas State Fair. Matthew, now 16, asked if he could wander off by himself, much to Henry's disappointment, but Mrs. Schaefer couldn't say no. Saying no to the boys for anything at that time was impossible.

The man operating the Roll-O-Plane pointed Matthew to the office of Midwest Big Shows, where Matthew lied about his age and procured a job with the carnival, after school and throughout the closing weekend. He would make 25 cents an hour and all the rides he wanted, as long as the trash was always picked up. One sighting of a cotton-candy paper cone or the remains of a dog-on-a-stick or snow-cone laying around for more than five minutes, and he's fired.

Matthew's mother was incapable of giving or denying permission in anything, so Matthew told Mrs. Schaefer about the job, and she told Daisy that she'd monitor Matthew, not to worry, which was ironic because Daisy was well past ever being worried about anything anymore.

So Matthew took the bus from school to the Fairgrounds every day at 3:30, went through the employee gate with his own pass and worked until midnight, getting a ride home from Gilbert, one of the roustabouts. On Saturday he took the bus from home to the Fairgrounds at 10 AM, and a midnight ride home with Gilbert. On Sunday, the last day of the fair, Matthew stayed after closing and helped break down the rides and the game and food stands, then hopped in the back of Gilbert's pickup with his heavy jacket, satchel of his few clothes, a photo of his Dad and Henry and him at Boyle's Kiddieland, and left Topeka. Midwest Big Shows' next stop was a weekend Fireman's Benefit in Lawrence, Kansas. And on from there, throughout the Midwest and beyond.

Early Monday morning, after the last day of the Fair, Henry knocked on Mrs. Schaefer's door before going to school.

"Yes Henry?" she answered the door. "Aren't you going to be late for school?"

"Oh, I won't be late, Mrs. Schaefer. The bus isn't here yet. Mrs. Schaefer, yesterday morning Matthew was putting his clothes in his bag before he went to the Fair. He didn't come home last night."

Mrs. Schaefer gasped. "Henry, did you tell your mother?"

"She's still asleep."

Mrs. Schaefer called the police, who went to the Grant home, woke up Mrs. Grant and told her what apparently happened. She simply told them "He's 16, let him go." She looked at Henry as if to ask, "Do you want to leave too?"

A Topeka detective drove to Midwest Big Shows in Lawrence where he found Matthew happily learning how to erect the Rock-O-Plane, lifting the two-seat compartments onto the wheel, using cotter pins to secure them. To the detective, the 16-year-old boy looked healthy, sounded alert and knew what he was doing. He had meals at the hamburger grill—he had to pay for his own candy and Cokes—a warm place to sleep, showers, and he made 25 cents an hour. The deal-closer for the detective was that Matthew was unofficially adopted by Ted Robinson, operator of the ride, married to a lady who worked a game joint. They convinced the detective that they'd take care of the kid, and after this show, he would be promoted from trash boy to assistant ride operator.

Satisfied, the detective reported back to Daisy Grant, who hardly cared. For his part, Henry was disappointed but entranced with Matthew's adventure. So encouraged, Henry got a job as a 14-year-old sweeping up the spilled popcorn in-between shows at The Grand Theater. He was there every day after school, staying until the last show was over at midnight, then walked home. On weekends he worked all day, his schoolbooks and notebook in hand so he could pass.

One of the movies at The Grand that Henry saw as many times as he could was 1947's "Nightmare Alley," about a young man, played by Tyrone Power, who joins a traveling carnival, comes to a sad end, and returns home. Maybe, Henry hoped, maybe, that would be Matthew, who after a year or two, would return home, knocking on the door the way their father did. But unlike their father, in Henry's movie-mind,

Matthew would stay, just like Tyrone Power did. Then his big brother would tell him all about his adventures of traveling with the carnival, which Henry was sure were just like Tyrone Power's.

KANSAS I-70 EAST
WILLARD 3
TOPEKA 21

Matthew jolted at the mileage sign, realizing he'd driven almost 70 miles without noticing the road, unaware of his foot on the accelerator; the radio talk program he'd ignored during his reverie had gone to static.

Topeka was only 21 miles away, but Matthew couldn't bear the thought of spending the night there. He took the Willard exit and found a cheap motel near the tracks, hoping the sound of the passing trains would lull him to sleep like when he was a boy. Instead, he had graphic dreams of the annihilation of Hiroshima, buildings leveled, people's faces ripped off, children slaughtered, and woke up to the crashing sound of the Kansas Pacific Freight Line outside the flimsy motel window.

When Matthew finally got back to sleep he was 16, in the back of the Robinsons' old pickup truck, clutching his jacket tight around him, on the road with Midwest Big Shows, heading nowhere.

THIRTEEN

Jenner, California, just 15 miles north of La Sangre, is where the Russian River, the largest tributary along the Northern California coast, finally meets and yields to the Pacific Ocean. At that juncture, on a bluff on the east side of Highway One, a restaurant has long sat. It served Russian food, appropriate given that Fort Ross was just twelve miles to the north. But people didn't necessarily go there for the food. It was the near-220 degree view of the Russian River and Pacific Ocean confluence that was unforgettable, be it in sunshine, fog, or rain, and always with the perfect sunset Diners left the restaurant saying "Oh yeah, and the food was good too!"

Every morning while waiting in the Spago Brothers Catering van for Gus and Deme to deliver the catch at Jenner's two-boat dock, Nicholas Spagopolous would gaze up at that restaurant on the bluff, and dream. He prayed that one day God in His Generosity would make that building the permanent home of Spago Brothers

Greek Restaurant. His brother Constantine would shrug—they had a highly successful restaurant in downtown Santa Rosa, plus the catering, let's be grateful for what we got—but when Nicholas mentioned it to Theresa she said No. Definitely Not. It was Wrong. Be grateful for our blessings, like Constantine says.

The family was getting used to Theresa's occasional declarations of truths, which she herself was learning to control. They certainly couldn't blame her for protecting something she had a financial interest in, and she did some investigation with the California Coastal Commission.

She discovered that since the CCC was formed after the restaurant was built, they could do little besides require petitions for any structural, color or signage changes; that iron regulation went for any pre-existing business along the Pacific Coast. As long as the owners made no exterior changes, they were good for life.

But Theresa saw a major earthquake, just waiting. It wasn't a specific vision, just a knowledge. One giant shrug of the San Andreas Fault could deposit that perched restaurant down onto Highway One, instantly transforming it from a sit-down restaurant into a drive-through. She shared this with Constantine and Nicholas, who shrugged and agreed that some dreams are better to just enjoy than to chase. Besides, the Russian Restaurant isn't going to leave; it could continue for generations.

The Russian Restaurant seemed to be the best place for Pastor William and Elizabeth Farrow to take a grieving Connie Satori for a friendly lunch. The District Office had asked the Farrows to stay on at La Sangre Christian Church, as a succession of various pastors is not what that crippled town needed right now. People were selling and leaving while the buyers were arriving, maintaining an almost-full church on Sunday mornings.

But Pastor Farrow was no fool, he knew that most of the newcomers crowded into the La Sangre Christian Church in an attempt to soak up the enigmatic energy they were convinced inhabited it. That's fine, Farrow figured, he'll have a captive audience from which perhaps one will hear.

"I'm glad we did this!" Elizabeth Farrow took in the view as they were given a window table. Her husband heartily agreed while Connie made a non-committal shrug and didn't look out the window. Instead, she studied the Farrows. William had a sprayed-solid Southern pompadour hair style and Elizabeth had a Nashville beehive; but apart from their We're Proud To Be Bible-Belters look, they weren't at all obnoxious. They spoke from the heart and Connie could find no fault in them. She could even appreciate their efforts, with her and with the church, but she wished she was just sitting at home, holding Freeman.

After the meal and the pleasant conversation, mostly about the Farrows getting adjusted to being back in the country after San Francisco, and carefully excluding children and family talk (which Elizabeth had so instructed William beforehand), they drove back to La Sangre. Connie gave a too-audible sigh of relief when they pulled up to her home. She thanked the Farrows, made a false promise of doing it again soon, and got out of the car, where she had sat alone in the back seat.

Inside she found Corey half-asleep in his father's recliner with the baby in the nearby playpen. Connie picked up Freeman and sat down in her chair. Lunch time.

Corey was getting used to watching his little brother being nursed. "How'd it go?" he asked his mother.

"What?"

"Lunch with the Farrows."

Connie looked at him blankly. "Where's Grace?"

"She went into Santa Rosa for some things, remember?"

"Santa Rosa?"

"Yes."

"For what things?"

"She needed some things for herself."

"Oh." Connie finally focused on Corey's face, and for a moment had to remember just who he was. It was her full grown son. A man.

"Mom?" Corey studied her.

"Yes, Corey?" she remembered.

His mother wasn't there.

Topeka Detective Donald Ellerbe unlocked one of the two heavy double-doors that flanked the ornate box office of the 1882 Grand Theater.

"There's a back door your brother uses," he told Matthew, "but he told me he wanted you to see the theater as you saw it as little boys, a last look before it gets torn down." Ellerbe gave Matthew a knowing look. "He wants to greet you inside. He told me it would be more like 'Citizen-Kane.' I don't know," Ellerbe shrugged, "I never saw that movie, before my time." He hesitated before opening the door. "Henry sure took good care of this place, anyway. Always vacuumed and shampooed the carpets, painted, repaired the seats. There were some locals who would donate money for his efforts, knowing the theater would never reopen, and damned if Henry didn't put every penny of the donations right into maintenance and repairs! And you know something Mr. Grant, he never smoked inside the theater. He'd stand out front, smoking and waving at people." Matthew read Ellerbe's look:

sad but not pathetic. "We all respect your brother, you know, and we all hate to see The Grand come down, but..." He opened the door and motioned Matthew through.

Just inside the Grand Theater door, 16-year-old Matthew handed the two tickets for him and Henry to the purple-uniformed usher inside the glamorous red-and-gold décor of The Grand Theater, in September of 1945. They were going to see "Back To Bataan," which Matthew vaguely knew was a bad idea, but 14-year-old Henry was insistent. "But Matthew, John Wayne's in it!" Matthew didn't know how to do what their parents used to do, just say no. And besides, they often went to the movies on Saturday afternoon, if they didn't go on a Friday night, and it didn't matter what was playing. In those days a child could see anything; they wouldn't understand it, they just enjoyed the visuals.

Matthew liked movies okay, but not matinees. He would sit through the Green Hornet serial, the previews, an occasional live performance, and the double feature, but he always felt free when they'd exit the theater and it was still daylight, the bright reality that Matthew so cherished. He'd just lost three or four hours of precious Kansas sun, windy or not.

But this time he should have told Henry, "We're not going to watch 'Back To Bataan.'" He should have taken him to the Orpheum Theater for "The Picture Of Dorian Gray" instead.

A little over three hours later, they walked the one mile home. Henry broke the silence.

"Hey Matthew?"

"Yeah?"

"Do you think Dad was in a prisoner of war camp, like in the movie?"

"I don't know. Mom got telegraphs from the War Department, but she didn't tell us what they said."

Henry considered that for a few minutes. "Remember at the beginning of the movie, all those guys are getting shot up?"

"Yeah."

"Do you think that could be how Dad lost his arm? In a battle?"

"Probably."

Henry pondered that. "That lady in the movie, the radio lady, she looked like the Japanese lady that Dad came home with."

"Yeah I know, she sounded like her too."

"Are Dad and that lady living in San Francisco now?"

"I guess so."

"Do you think we'll ever see Dad again?"

"I don't know, Henry."

"Matthew!" An unfamiliar middle-aged male voice resonated through the plush, dimly-lit lobby of the current day Grand Theater. 51-year-old Henry Grant walked down the red-carpeted staircase from the mezzanine. "So good to see you Matthew! It's been a long time!"

Henry was a few inches shorter than Matthew, stockier but with no extra weight. He was well-groomed, wearing a polo shirt with pocket holding a pack of Marlboros, pressed khakis, and well-shined oxfords. Matthew would have walked right past him on the street; but then what should he expect after 37 years? But whereas Matthew had the harshly-lined, sun-burnt, stubbly face of a lifetime carny, Henry's face was clean-shaven, smooth and youthful, apparently still unused in the real world. His brown hair had only mild touches of gray, and was well trimmed.

Henry's greeting sounded sincere, his walk down the steps towards Matthew was steady enough, and yet somehow it all looked and sounded like a scene from a movie, "Citizen Kane" apparently. Maybe it was the setting, the aged yet clean opulence of the lobby, the large, arched stained-glass window above the entrance creating film-noirish lighting throughout. The fixtures at the refreshment counter were polished and sparkling; one would correctly assume the restrooms were the same.

Matthew found himself wondering what his greeting should be. "Same here, Henry," he said, stepping forward. What should he do? Handshake? Hug? What?

Henry looked Matthew in the eyes as he extended his hand for an overdone shake. Henry's expression was basic and simple: it was of awe and pride in his prodigal big brother. "You look like Gary Cooper," Henry said admiringly, not taking his eyes off Matthew's.

"Yeah, well," Matthew shrugged, "some people have told me that."

"The way you...I mean the way Cooper was all alone in that town, in 'High Noon,' no one supported him, and he was the Marshall. Remember when he knocked on his Deputy's door, hoping he'll join him in a gunfight against the bad guys, and the Deputy's wife lied for him and said he wasn't home, when the Deputy was hiding in the bedroom? Cooper was all alone. He faced the bad guys all alone. That's what you look like."

Matthew didn't know what to do with that, didn't know what to say, so he looked around. "The place looks just like when we were boys, just as big as I remember."

"Wait until you see the theater," Henry grinned. "Come on." He led the way through the set of red doors into the auditorium. Matthew turned back to Ellerbe, who just waved at him and left the theater, locking the front door.

If the lobby looked just as big as Matthew remembered, the 1300-seat auditorium looked even bigger, the balcony higher and grander, even the slightly tattered stage curtains were still luxurious. The Grand Theater was ready, waiting, for the lights to dim and the projectionist to roll the ads for local merchants and the theater's refreshment stand offering popcorn, candy, and Cokes.

Henry walked down the left aisle to the screen, and pointed at the front row center. "Remember when we saw 'Back to Bataan,' Matthew? We sat right there. I remember cause I thought we were actually inside that movie, in the war, where Dad was. I was so scared I had my hands over my eyes. But," he smiled at Matthew, "I'd stopped jumping in your bed by then."

Matthew looked down, in failure. He *wanted to want* to love Henry but he didn't want to. If he did, he'd be embracing everything that happened in their lives, and face the fact that his own life was a lie, an act, a Jack Kareouc fantasy that he sold to himself, and obviously to his little brother.

Matthew, didn't you also sell that act to Lillian? At the 1962 Seattle World's Fair?

"What, Matthew?" Henry was perplexed at Matthew looking down at the floor. "Is there something wrong? Did I say the wrong t hing?"

Matthew couldn't answer. Admitting to yourself, in your fifties, that you're a fraud can be a real pain in the ass.

FOURTEEN

Doyle could still feel Theresa's touch, her hand enveloped in his. It inspired him, drove him in his work, and as such he came in first for vehicular output from the Service Department at Emerald Ford.

But Line Manager Dean admonished him. "Hey Seeno, don't go *too* fast. Don't forget, if you don't do it right the first time, it'll come back to you!"

Returns were a black mark against the mechanics, and Emerald Ford adopted President Reagan's Comprehensive Crime Control Act of 1984, AKA Three-Strikes-And-You're-Out. But none of Doyle's vehicles came back.

The young Doyle Seeno was back. He was fifty years old, still living in La Sangre, California, and yet he was now back to the happy, innocent, hopeful, trusting young boy in McCarthy, Texas. While the abuse he suffered there could never be forgotten, it didn't color his life anymore. It was his choice to either dwell in it, or to hold onto the memories of his otherwise wonderful childhood.

His favorite pastime was wandering the fields with his Brittany Spaniel, Rex, bee-bee gun in hand. He shot a rabbit only once, and after the rabbit looked Doyle in the eye as it accepted its slow, painful death, Doyle never shot another. Besides, Rex did all the rabbit killing, which Doyle's mother soaked in red wine overnight and served with rice. Still, he carried his gun as all the other boys did. He graduated to a .22, which his father proudly bought him for his 12th birthday, but Doyle just used it for target practice, confiscating all his Mom's empty tin cans, and he became a good shot. Not a hunter maybe, but a good shot.

At 13, Doyle started hanging around Dusty's Garage after school and on weekends, doing odd jobs such as cleanup and repairing tires. He watched, learned, and handed tools to old Dusty as he worked on the early 1930s Fords and Chevys. ("Ford makes a better truck!" Dusty advised Doyle.) At closing time, when Doyle had to go home for supper, Dusty would shake Doyle's hand, slipping him a 50-cent piece, saying "Good job today Boy!" The next year Doyle enrolled in McCarthy High School's Automotive classes, where he earned all A's.

Now, after getting the job with Emerald Ford and meeting Maria, Doyle could say that he actually had a fun childhood in Texas: its big sky, the easy engagement of its people, all memorably engulfed him. He was able to push all that other crap aside. Doyle Seeno was back, ready to resume—or rather start—his life.

And now he had plenty to do. First off, he thanked Lillian and told her he wouldn't need her and Julie to help him set up an apartment. He was going to stay in La Sangre after all, in his room above the garage.

"Why?" Lillian asked him. "I mean, you're not going to get an apartment in Santa Rosa?"

"Well, I'm making plans, Lillian. Not exactly sure what they are yet. Big changes are happening, that's all I really know."

Lillian smiled at him, happy for him, suddenly realizing that he was a far cry from the confused man who used to stiffly addressed her as "Nurse Walker." But then, why didn't she ever correct him, allow him to address her by her Christian name?

It was because you felt superior to him, and you patronized him, Lillian.

Everything in Doyle's new life, his new awareness, his new vision, coming full circle with himself, was now all centered around Theresa. He sat with all the others in the lunch room at Emerald City Ford and listened to their cheery talk but could only think about Theresa, her firm working hand inside his calloused, working hand. Every car he worked on, every socket wrench he touched, every tightening and loosening he made, every spark plug he changed, every brake shoe he replaced, was all about Theresa. He'd finish working on a car, drive it out to the customer, get out and remove the protective driver seat covering, thank the customer, and knew that very car would soon be driving the same Sonoma County roads as Theresa's olive green BMW.

Doyle had just gotten home from work, parked his truck behind the La Sangre Gas Station, and went around to the front to ask Micah if the gas shipment arrived on time, when he saw Theresa drive into town. She honked and waved, and while the wave was for Doyle and Micah, Doyle took it for himself as he crossed the One to the dirt road leading down to the homes.

"Doyle?" Micah called after him, but Doyle vaguely heard him and waved him off. Nothing mattered but seeing Theresa again, to hold her hand again. He was going to where he belonged. He knocked on the door of Theresa's new home.

"Hi."

"Hello."

"I just thought...I mean I saw you drive in...."

"I saw you too."

"I know," Doyle said, his voice lower and softer than before, "you honked and waved. I just thought...you might need help moving."

Theresa didn't answer right away, trying to understand her feeling. With her gift-switch permanently on in La Sangre, she was afraid it might be interfering with reality, creating a false filter for what she thought was a true feeling. Was this strange, scary-in-an-exciting-way feeling for Doyle real, or was it La Sangre-charged?

It was real. As Theresa stood in the doorway, her attraction to this man and her gift were one and the same, and not despite La Sangre, but, strangely, *because* of La Sangre. There was no contradiction, the two were hand in hand, as she and Doyle were at The La Sangre Last Chance Gas Station on...when was that? Yesterday? A year ago? All her life?

"I, uh..." she backed into the house to allow him to enter, "I just moved in all the kitchen stuff, it's still in boxes, but I can grab a few things and throw something together for us to have dinner. There's some things in the fridge I can throw in a pot. Would you like that? I'm a great cook."

Doyle nodded, suddenly dry-mouthed. "That would be nice. But if you don't mind, I'd like a glass of water first, please."

"Of course."

As he followed Theresa inside he knew he had finally, at last, found himself. The young Doyle Seeno was completely back.

It was another busy day in the Santa Rosa General Hospital ER, but Julie and Lillian still found time to meet at the smoking area in the parking lot, where they could be alone. Lillian sensed that Julie needed to talk, she'd noticed it in the ER. Now on break, Lillian decided instead of waiting for Julie to start, she'll bring up something mundane.

"Did I mention that Doyle won't be getting an apartment after all. He won't need our help."

"Is he going to keep living over the gas station?"

"I guess so. 'La Sangre is his home,' that's what he told me."

Julie pondered it. "Poor man, this is probably the first real home he's ever had. He's shared with all of us in church about the years of wandering from that horrid small town in Texas. Kind of like..." she caught herself.

"Kind of like Matthew?" Lillian asked her, not surprised.

"I'm sorry, I didn't mean..."

"Oh no Julie, I've thought about that many times. Interesting that Matthew and Doyle are such a similar type, tall and thin, but they used to look decidedly different. Now they're looking almost like brothers, haven't you noticed?"

Julie looked at her. "I *thought* something was different about Doyle! Whereas Matthew hasn't changed a bit."

That statement was unintentionally loaded, but Lillian ignored it. She couldn't indulge herself talking about doubts she was now having about her husband, she was here for Julie, and she had to wait for Julie to start. So she waited, looking at the butts in the concrete receptacle, understanding why people smoke.

"Lillian," Julie began tentatively, "I only know one way to say it: I don't know my husband, not since he signed on with that writer's agency."

Lillian gave Julie a chance to continue, when she didn't, she chose an innocent question. "When is his book coming out?"

"They told him August."

"That's awfully quick, isn't it? Are you sure it isn't just because Nathan's so busy, thinking about nothing but his book?"

"Oh there's some of that I guess. But that book has changed the whole dynamic of our marriage. I used to be able to read Nathan, but now...he's not there, or worse, I don't think I know who he *is!*"

Lillian mused. She and Matthew were going to celebrate their First Anniversary in September. If their honeymoon was over, it was when they kissed good-bye right here in the parking lot/smoking area. She wondered if she spoke too soon about telling Matthew to bring his poor brother to La Sangre. The empty room above the La Sangre Garage was why she agreed so readily to Matthew bringing Henry back; she wouldn't have let Henry into their tiny cottage, and Matthew would have understood.

"You're very lucky," Julie turned to Lillian. "Matthew is the kind of man that's right in your face, you know where he's coming from."

"Lately I'm not so sure about that." Lillian didn't mean to let that out.

"Lillian? Why do you say that?"

Lillian had wanted to keep the attention on Julie, but maybe Julie had said all she could at this time. "Well, Matthew called me from Topeka this morning, and he didn't sound good."

"Not good? Something to do with his brother?"

"I don't know, and I didn't ask."

"You didn't ask?"

Lillian shook her head. Yes, this is why people smoked. "No, I don't ask him anything. He's a man who has an incredible need for space. I have to let him be." She paused. "Looking back at Seattle in '62, I can't believe how I pestered him. I was all over him. I'm surprised I didn't scare him away."

But you did Lillian, or don't you remember?

"Lillian," Julie entreated, "you were only nineteen!"

"Young and dumb," Lillian agreed. "Anyway I've begun to think there may be two Matthews, one is the showman on the road, the other is the stay-at-home, and maybe he's just been playing at the latter for the past year. Perhaps I underestimated just how powerful a hold the road may still have on him. More powerful than mine, I'm afraid."

KANSAS I-70 WEST
DENVER 540
SALT LAKE CITY 1048

Matthew and Henry had just gotten on the freeway after leaving Topeka, the trunk full with hundreds of flat, stacked movie posters, over a hundred Beta and VHS tapes and their respective machines, and the back seat holding the Grand Theater's antique brass-and-glass popcorn machine. Their personal belongings were somehow crammed in the remaining spaces.

Henry tapped a couple of cigarettes out of his Marlboro pack. "Want one?"

Matthew hadn't smoked in almost twenty years, but he had to do something for this long trip. "Yeah, sure."

Henry put two cigarettes in his lips, lit them and handed one to Matthew. "So Matthew, did you see 'Nightmare Alley?'"

Matthew shook his head and took a drag. Henry had brought up so many movies in the last 24 hours as he packed his spartan clothes and said good-bye to The Grand, that Matthew realized he himself hardly ever saw movies. Most small town movie theaters closed at midnight, when the carnival closed, and after 14 straight hours of hustling rides, the last thing Matthew wanted to do was clean up and go to a late night movie, unless it was for some balcony romance with a girl he met at the carnival, in which case, who saw the film?

"Well," Henry went on, "'Nightmare Alley' came out right after you left." Whenever Henry mentioned his big brother's absence, he did so with ease, like it was a non-issue, just a happenstance. "And I knew you were out traveling with the carnivals, just like Tyrone Power did in that movie." He turned to Matthew. "You were Tyrone Power, but you don't look like him, you're still Gary Cooper. Did you see him in 'The Court-Martial of Billy Mitchell?'"

"No."

"Well Coop was in that, but that was about World War I, and I don't like war films, not after we saw 'Back To Bataan.'"

Matthew wondered if he should pursue that, but he didn't get the chance.

"When Mom died in 1957..." Henry began.

Where was I in 1957? Matthew wondered. What show was I working? I don't remember where I was or what I was doing when my own mother died.

"...the movie 'Sayonara' came out, and I don't like war movies but I saw the poster, and it was about Marlon Brando and Red Buttons who both fall in love with Japanese women during World War II, and Red Buttons marries his girl. Did you see it?"

"Uh...no."

"Well I thought that's what happened to Dad, maybe he met a Japanese girl and fell in love with her, and if he was alone and away during the war, maybe I can see how that happened. But you know, the lady who played Red Buttons' wife, her name is Miyoshi Umeki." He turned to Matthew, whose eyes were crinkled, not knowing where this might go or what he should say. "Matthew, that's the name of the Japanese lady that Dad brought home after the war! Except she changed it to Mia, remember? But I thought maybe it was Dad's Miyoshi, and she had become a movie star! Do you remember when Mia said 'If my husband wants me to work for him, I will.' So I thought maybe she got work as an actress. But when I watched the movie I could see it wasn't the same lady, it didn't look like her, and Dad's Miyoshi spoke perfect English, didn't she?"

"Yes. She did."

"So I think I understand why Dad did that, fell in love with a Japanese lady, don't you Matthew?"

"I guess so," Matthew replied. And it killed our Mother.

Like you did with Lillian? Leaving her in Seattle without saying good-bye? At least your father came home to say good-bye, even if he didn't say a word.

"So Matthew, did that happen to you in Korea? Did you meet a Korean girl?"

"No, I didn't...I mean, I didn't serve."

"Oh really? I was classified 4-F, you know, just like Jerry Lewis on 'Which Way To The Front.'"

"Yeah, I was 4-F too."

Stop lying Matthew! You were working for West Coast Shows in 1951, right when the Korean War broke out. WCS had a booking at the Pacific National Exposition in Vancouver BC. You were always fit, you were 1-A material, so when the PNE ended, instead of returning to the states with WCS, you got on with Royal Canadian Shows and crossed the continent several times with them. In fact your Canadian ID was the first form of personal identification you ever had; you had to get one because RCS wouldn't pay you in cash like the American shows did. Two years later, in fall of '53, you returned to the U.S., finally got a Social Security Card and opened a bank account. You steered clear of the Korean War, and when the Vietnam War broke out nine years later, you were too old, so you worked the Seattle World's Fair, where you met Lillian.

Yes. Lillian. You were pretty ingenious when you met up again a year ago at the Santa Rosa hospital, telling her that you left her in Seattle without saying good-bye because you were upset that she got an abortion without talking to you about it. Bullshit, Grant! You didn't *want* her traveling with you, you wanted to go back out alone, and her getting pregnant trapped you. Then she got an abortion, which was your get-out-of-jail-free card. You were freed of any obligation. You jumped on the truck as soon as the Wild Mouse was dismantled, and didn't even have the human decency to tell that nice lady good-bye. So you're a liar *and* a draft dodger! Now, can you play the cool, existential, freewheeling dude while facing a World War II, Korean, or Vietnam vet?

"Oh stop!" Matthew cried out loud, then hurriedly added "Oh no, not you Henry. I was just thinking about something."

"That's funny," Henry laughed. "You sounded just like Jimmy Stewart in 'Bell, Book, and Candle,' when he's riding in a taxi and you hear him wondering about whether or not Kim Novak is really a witch, and he says 'Oh stop!' and the cab driver stops, and Stewart says 'Oh no, not you.' Did you see that movie, Matthew?"

"Uh, sorry, what's the name of the movie?"

"'Bell, Book and Candle,' 1958."

"No."

Henry kept on. "So Matthew, I can't believe we're going to be living right near Bodega Bay, that is so great! I still have 'The Birds' poster, and you know, if you think you can really get me a job in the La Sangre Antique Store, I can put some of my old posters up in the store, just like I did in The Grand the last few years. The poster that everyone really liked was 'Attack Of The 50 Foot Woman' and...."

Matthew took a deep drag of his cigarette. Ah yes. Thank you God for nicotine. His resumed smoking habit should be the least of Lillian's concern that the road might bring back his old habits. Hell. he barely looked at other women over the past year, she'll just have to accept the smoking. As he had agreed when they reunited at the hospital, he'll smoke outside the house, carry Altoids with him, pop two before he kisses her, and wonder why he stopped smoking in the first place.

"....and that one I could sell for probably a thousand dollars...Matthew?"

"What? Oh, yeah Henry, those movie posters of yours should sell for a lot of money," Matthew lamely tried to continue the conversation...if that's what it was.

"Oh no Matthew, my posters are just for show. I'll never sell them. But there's a guy in

Hollywood, Eric Caidin is his name, and he owns a store called 'Hollywood Book and Poster,' right on Hollywood Boulevard. From him I can buy eight-by-ten black-and-white press photos. I can buy some of 'The Birds,' do photo-copies of each one and sell them for $10 each. Maybe I could get Tippi Hedren to sign them, they could sell for $50. Or maybe I can turn them into post-cards, don't you think? Do they have postcards of 'The Birds' in Bodega Bay?"

"Not that I've seen."

"Well, The Tides Restaurant is still there, right? I could sell post cards to them in bulk and they can resell them at a profit. I heard that whenever 'The Birds' is shown on TV people swarm to Bodega Bay and The Tides Restaurant."

That was certainly true, people would indeed buy those postcards. ("Having a wonderful time, The Birds are attacking!") They swarmed to both The Tides and the old Bodega Bay School House, home movie cameras ready, waiting and hoping for a bird attack.

From his own carnival background, Matthew couldn't deny that Henry was enterprising and seemed to know the value of selling small items like photos or postcards. Hell, such items were given as prizes at the game joints in the shows he worked. Spend seven dollars on darts and you might win a 50-cent, 8x10 unlicensed photo of the latest singing sensation, Madonna, with a fake autograph no less. As P. T. Barnum famously gospelized, "There's a sucker born every minute."

Corey had told Matthew that Henry's room would be rent-free, as was Doyle's. And after seeing how responsible Henry was with The Grand, Matthew would have to suggest to Corey that Henry work at the Antique Store; after all, the couple who ran it were leaving La Sangre.

Yeah, Henry will be fine, as far as all that goes. But Matthew was deeply afraid he might be making yet a second serious mistake with his little brother.

La Sangre is not a healthy environment for a 53-year-old child.

KANSAS I-70 WEST
DENVER 500
SALT LAKE CITY 1008

They'd only gone 40 miles so far. Was Matthew going to make this trip without killing Henry, or himself? Or at least smoking a carton of Marlboros? Ironic that Matthew's own cig of choice since he first joined the carnival was Marlboro. Ted Robinson offered him his first at 16. Matthew relished operating the Rock-O-Plane with a cigarette dangling from his mouth. ("Just don't throw the butt on the sawdust, Matt!")

"Hey Matthew, this reminds me of 'National Lampoon's Vacation,' you know, when Chevy Chase and his family are driving across the country, on their way to Wally World, and they stop at a...."

SEPTEMBER - DECEMBER, 1985

FIFTEEN

TRANSCRIPT
THE BILL DUNAWAY SHOW
SEPTEMBER 1, 1985

COMMERCIAL BREAK (Visine, Casio Watches, Gillette) & STATION ID.

BILL DUNAWAY:
We're back, with Nathan Steer, author of *The Secret of La Sangre*; Feminist Jane Sorenson, author of *It Ends Now: The Victimization of Women*; and Dr. Ralph Owen, Psychiatrist. We've been discussing the Father's Day murders in La Sangre, California. Ms. Sorenson, let's go to you. As we know, Maria Malana has been charged with First Degree Murder, but you believe that charge should be dropped. Do you mean that a lesser charge such as Second Degree Murder or Manslaughter would be acceptable? After all, Malana's lawyer has stipulated that she paid Bruno Logges, a bodyguard, to murder her father as well as Dr. Owen here, although the bodyguard ended up killing Pastor Salvatore Satori instead.

JANE SORENSON:
Well let me start by saying that Ms. Malana did *not* murder

anyone, she simply defended herself and society by murdering the man, her very own father, who raped her, as well as her own daughter and sister. What might that man have done if Ms. Malana hadn't had him executed?

DUNAWAY:
'Executed?' Not murdered?

SORENSON:
That's right Bill. Malana had her father executed. What if she hadn't? Would her father be cruising schoolyards in San Francisco, or anywhere else for that matter? Ms. Malana simply put a stop to him to protect the rest of us.

(AUDIENCE APPLAUSE)

DUNAWAY:
But couldn't this or shouldn't this have been put in the hands of the law?

SORENSON:
The law, Bill? What does the law ever do about it? If you don't have bruises or photographs or witnesses or even a video of the crime, the men get off free, because you can't prove anything in court. They do it in secret, the victim has no proof, they get off free, while we have to suffer the consequences and live in constant fear.

DUNAWAY:
Dr. Owen, I know you can't discuss the upcoming case, but you are a witness for the defense, and in fact you once treated Jessie Malana, the daughter and sister of the defendant. And even though you were Maria Malana's

intended victim, you're an expert witness for her defense! What say you about Ms. Sorenson's assertion?

DR. RALPH OWEN:
First of all, everyone has to be held accountable for their crimes, but I understand what Ms. Sorenson is asking, was this actually a crime?

SORENSON:
I'm not *asking* if it's a crime, Doctor, I'm *saying* it isn't a crime.

(AUDIENCE APPLAUSE)

DUNAWAY:
Dr. Owen, you were saying...

OWEN:
Well, crimes of passion are ignited by rage, usually stemming from some type of abuse in the past or present, and within the grip of passion and rage, the victim of the abuse can sometimes do things they'd never consider doing.

DUNAWAY:
Doctor, could what you describe be the basis for an insanity plea?

OWEN:
Rage is powerful, and it can drive people to do the wrong thing, but it's very unlikely that even within the iron grip of their rage, a person would not know that what they're doing is wrong. They know it's wrong but they can't help themselves, and that doesn't support a plea of insanity.

But I do want to say is that if someone has been raped or sexually abused, they're never going to be the same as if it hadn't happened. They have to learn to live through the trauma, try to put it behind them, and to forgive.

SORENSON:
Forgive? You mean you expect Ms. Malana, or any other female victim, to *forgive* her rapist?

(AUDIENCE APPLAUSE)

DUNAWAY:
I don't know if that applause is for or against forgiveness. Doctor, what do you think?

OWEN:
Well if you don't at least try to forgive someone else, you're not hurting them at all, but you're tearing yourself up inside. I've had a lot of patients that are so locked in their hate and blood-thirst for revenge—even after the perpetrator is given a life sentence or executed—that they become developmentally frozen and cut themselves off from living a fuller, happier life.

DUNAWAY:
Let's take some questions from the audience.

WOMAN AUDIENCE MBR #1
Thank you, this is for Mr. Steer. I read your book, *The Secret Of La Sangre*,...

NATHAN STEER:
Thank you!

WOMAN #1:
...and I was hoping that perhaps forgiveness would be the secret of all that's happened in that town. But I didn't really see that throughout the book. If you don't mind my asking, are you an atheist?

(SILENCE)

DUNAWAY:
Mr. Steer? Do you mind the question, are you an atheist?

NATHAN STEER:
Uh no, I don't mind the question. I'm open-minded. Just show me some proof and I'll consider a God, but you sure wouldn't know it by the people in that town.

WOMAN #1:
Then why are you living there?\

STEER:
I...well...I'm a journalist. And I moved there to uncover the secret of La Sangre.

WOMAN:
So, what's the secret?

(LONG SILENCE)

DUNAWAY:
Let's take another question. Yes sir, coming right over.

Nathan Steer discovered that one second on television is like a minute. He assumed that his long hesitation would be edited, but it wasn't. It was an extended closeup shot of him sitting there, dumbfounded with the question. What should have been his moment of triumph, appearing as an author on "The Bill Dunaway Show," was a national humiliation. Fortunately for him, that embarrassing moment was overshadowed by the protesters outside.

TRANSCRIPT
ABC NIGHTLY NEWS WITH PERRY SWANSON
SEPTEMBER 1, 1985

PERRY SWANSON:
Good evening everyone. The mysterious and enigmatic town of La Sangre, California is back in the news, as Maria Malana, who allegedly paid a killer to murder two people, her father and Psychiatrist Ralph Owen, has been charged with murder. Sandra Billings, our associate from Santa Rosa, California, and who has been following La Sangre since the turmoil originally began in June of 1984, is outside the WNBC Studios here in New York City.

SANDRA BILLINGS:
(CHANTING IN BACKGROUND, "FREE MARIA! FREE MARIA!")
Good evening Perry. The Bill Dunaway Show is currently being taped here, and there's quite a crowd of protesters demanding that Maria Malana not be charged with any crime. I've asked a few of the people why they think she shouldn't be tried for murder, despite her own confession.

WOMAN #1:
I'd like to know where the law was when Maria was being raped as a child. But now they show up to charge her with murder. What is the matter with the police? They're supposed to protect us, but all they do is prosecute us!

WOMAN #2:
Freeing Maria would send a clear message to men that they can not get away with this!

WOMAN #3:
Maria is *not* a murderess, she is a victim, and, I believe, a survivor!

Watching Nathan on Bill Dunaway, Julie Steer was mortified as much for herself as for her husband.

Corey didn't tell his mother about the show, though he watched it in the Owens' cottage. Corey had picked up Dr. Owen from the San Francisco Airport, returning from the Dunaway taping. After the airing, Corey thanked Dr. Owen for his professionalism and his stalwart support of Maria, and his father, Sal.

Anne Owen was pissed off that her husband never mentioned her name or her own book, *Murder By The Sea: The True Story of La Sangre*. Dunaway didn't mention it in his introduction of Ralph, and Anne didn't doubt that her husband had instructed Dunaway not to do so.

For his part, Ralph wasn't particularly impressed with being on the Dunaway Show, nor that, next week, his wife was scheduled to appear on the new "Olive Gentry Show." Gentry was the Wonder Woman from Atlanta who was touted as Bill Dunaway's new formidable rival. Actually, Anne Owen wasn't impressed with Gentry, whom she thought was fat and obnoxious and not as smart as Dunaway. Still, Anne Owen swore off Bill Dunaway and joined the growing legion of Olive Gentry fans.

The most fun with the Dunaway show on La Sangre was had by Maria Malana's cronies in the Sacramento County Jail, as they whooped and cheered throughout the broadcast, while the guards continually warned them to pipe down or they'll turn the TV off.

"I think we can talk the DA down to Second Degree Murder," Maria's lawyer told her and Ralph in the prison's private conference room.

"Second degree," Maria scoffed. "What good does that do?"

"Quite a bit, Maria," her lawyer didn't hide his impatient tone. He was a good lawyer, well-respected, expensive, and in enough demand that he could indulge expressing his impatience with the woman who became his most difficult client. "The way California law is written, for now," he emphasized, "is that with Murder

Two you can possibly get paroled after only seven years, given good behavior. There are opponents wanting to abolish that law, especially in these Reagan tough-on-crime years, so let's strike before they succeed."

"Seven years," Maria mumbled.

"Maria..." Ralph implored.

"Yes, seven years," her lawyer looked at her firmly, "if you behave yourself. And that means no smart-ass remarks to the guards, and no walking through the cell block yelling 'Eat your horny hearts out, you lezzies!'"

Maria was quiet, though maintained her petulance.

"Come on Maria," Ralph practically pleaded.

"Oh all right, you assholes. I'll do it."

Her lawyer looked at Ralph; it was a triumph of sorts. "See that you do," he looked back at Maria.

"BUT I WON'T LIKE IT!"

Ralph suppressed a chuckle, grateful he had a sense of humor about the woman who tried to kill him. He and her lawyer studied Maria. The lady was beautiful, smart, and a real pistol with a great sense of humor, but they were both too old and experienced to lose their heads over her, though they could certainly see why a young, naive Corey Satori easily did so.

"And," her lawyer pointed at her in finality,

"I am *not* putting you on the fucking witness stand!"

Thanks to the adroit handling of her Christian public defender, Ruby was not charged as an accessory to murder. The State's Attorney was satisfied that she was an innocent dupe, and that she really did nothing to aid Maria in her revenge; she just sent Maria letters about idle gossip in La Sangre, and was truly under the impression that all Maria wanted from her was to introduce Maria to Dr. Owen so she could discuss Jessie's suicide with him.

Still, when the Judge advised Ruby during the inquest that she would not be charged, he told her bluntly to "get your own life and stop gossiping about others, or one day you'll flap your jaw to the wrong person, and you may not be so lucky. I respect and appreciate your chosen faith, Miss Rogers, but you really should read James, Chapter 3." He slammed the gavel.

September 5, 1985

Dear Ruby,

I just got your letter, and I'm glad you're not being charged for the crime of conspiracy to murder. But if you think you can move in with me and Dennis and the kids in order to as you say "Get back to my roots and form a good relationship with me," you are grossly mistaken.

You were always the cute one, the vivacious one and I was the smart but ugly sister. Well I got married and my husband has a good job and he makes a lot of money as Floor Manager of Harrah's Club in South Lake Tahoe. We just bought a home in Carson City and yes we have a guest room but you're going to have to "find yourself" somewhere else, not here. Mom and Dad left you the La Sangre house because they figured that unlike me your "ugly sister" you'll never get married or have children. They were right weren't they. You were cute and funny but it wore off quickly. So you can just live off your house in La Sangre, you deserve it. You and I knew as kids that town was crazy, so I left it and got on with my life while you got the house and stayed there and obviously went crazy like everyone else. It's just like that country song "She got the goldmine and I got the shaft." So enjoy all the money you're making off the house and please let me live my own very happy life.

Oh and to answer your question, no, your niece and nephew never ask about you, their "Crazy Aunt Ruby."

Your sister in memory,
Rose

TRANSCRIPT
THE OLIVE GENTRY SHOW
SEPTEMBER 15, 1985

COMMERCIAL BREAK (Blue Cross, Johnson & Johnson, Tampax) & STATION ID.

OLIVE GENTRY:
We're back with Mrs. Anne Owen, author of the best selling paperback book, *Murder By The Sea: The True Story Of La Sangre*. Mrs. Owen, in your book you claim that the town of La Sangre itself is (READS FROM BOOK) "...full of evil. I never could understand where that came from, but it had a very adverse effect on all the people there." Now how did you and your husband not succumb to what you describe as a "very toxic environment."

ANNE OWEN:
Well Olive, as I said in my book *Murder By The Sea: The True Story of La Sangre*, my husband and I only summered there after we bought the home ten years ago. We didn't go to their church and didn't socialize with them, of course they're not the kind of people you could call social. Actually they were downright rude to us, and they all believed that psychiatrists and psychologists are the (MAKES QUOTATION MARKS WITH FINGERS) "spawn of Satan."

GENTRY:
Then, why did you stay there?

OWEN:
Oh, it's so beautiful Olive, by the ocean! Have you ever

been there?

GENTRY:
No.

OWEN: Well it really is beautiful! Even if the people are a little strange.

GENTRY:
Strange in what way? Besides not trusting psychiatrists.

OWEN:
Well after all Olive, there have been four deaths there in a year's time. For a town with a population of one hundred, don't you think that's a little strange?

GENTRY:
But I don't understand. I was raised in the church, I've experienced both sincere people and...extremists. Were the La Sangre people legalistic?

OWEN:
Well, they didn't drink or dance or any of that, but they... well all the time I was around them...I felt like an outsider, like I was judged, or not good enough.

GENTRY:
Did they threaten you?

OWEN:
Well...no.

GENTRY:
So, I'm not clear on what you're angry about.

OWEN:
I'm not angry! I just think that the truth has to be told!

GENTRY:
And just what is the truth?

OWEN:
Well Olive, as I said in my book *Murder By The Sea: The True Story of La Sangre*, it was a very toxic place!

GENTRY:
(LETS OUT BREATH) Let's take another break.

Ralph Owen watched his wife on "The Olive Gentry Show" when it aired three days after the taping, while Anne continued her two-week media tour booked by the publisher, doing local morning shows, newspaper interviews, and nighttime radio talk shows in the major markets.

As Ralph watched his wife's embarrassing turn on national TV, he remembered meeting her when she was Anne Sullivan, an English Major at the University of California at San Francisco. She was young, bright, cute and funny, and her goal as a college student was to write a book, though she didn't know about what. ("Something that can help change the world," she told him on their first date.) To this day Ralph wasn't sure if he ever fell in love with

Anne, but he did get her pregnant after a couple of dates. He then did the right thing, as he was raised, and he married her. They produced two just-off-center children—Ralph now attributed that to his staunch atheism—while he became an excellent and successful psychiatrist. As his own marriage somehow carried on, his biggest challenge as a psychiatrist was in dealing with married couples with their children grown and gone, to whom he was tempted to just advise "forgive each other, get a divorce, and get on with your separate lives while you still can."

"You were good, Annie," Ralph kissed her at the San Francisco Airport when she returned from the tour, "on the Olive Show, I mean. Did they give you tapes of your other local shows?"

"Oh yes!" she glowed. "But they're all on VHS. Can you buy a VHS machine so we can watch them together? Ours is just that old Beta."

"Sure Hon."

"Hello?"

"Hey Julie!" Nathan's voice boomed over the phone. "Guess where I am!"

She was finding it more difficult to feign enthusiasm. What scared her is that Nathan didn't even know she was faking it, in or out of the bedroom. "I don't know, Nathan, where are you?"

"I'm at a pay phone in the lobby of—hold on—the *Black Tower*!"

(The Black Tower?) "The Black Tower?" she asked aloud.

"Yes, the Universal friggin' Black Tower Jules! I was just up there with—hold on tighter babe—my agent and *Stu Waterman*!"

She was late on her response. "Oh, that's wonderful Nathan. You actually got to meet him?"

"Yeah, in this big boardroom with a polished mahogany table about a mile long. Abe and I were at one end and Stu—Mr. Waterman—was at the other end with four—count 'em—four lawyers in Armani suits! I wish you could have seen it, Jules!"

"Well...." Julie could have taken the time off and gone to LA with Nathan, but Nathan's invitation was an afterthought; besides, there's no way any wife would be invited to a high-powered meeting like that. She'd just be waiting in the lobby watching people go by, wondering if they were famous but not caring.

"Julie baby, you should hear what they're talking about! Mr. Waterman said he's talking to ABC-TV about making my book a mini-series. A *mini-series* Jules!"

"That's great Hon!"

"Yeah, it's better than a movie cause it'll be six hours long instead of just two, They'll be able to keep my whole book in, not chop it up."

"Did Abe ask Waterman if you can write the screenplay?"

"Naw. He said that would be pushing it for a first time author. Anyway it needs the Hollywood touch, editing the story to fit in with commercial breaks, that kind of stuff. But wait til you hear the names he suggested for the cast: David Soul as Pete Freeman, Desi Arnaz Jr. as Sal Satori, Florence Henderson as Connie Satori, Cloris Leachman as Lillian, William Katt as Corey, Henry Winkler as Matthew, Dennis Weaver as Doyle, Valerie Bertinelli as Maria, Jodie Foster as Jessie, Ed Asner as Ralph, Lucille Ball as Ruby—remember? I told you that Ruby has Lucille Ball hair—and, drum roll, guess who he sees playing me?"

"Woody Allen?"

"Stop it Julie! No, for me it's either Matt Dillon or John Cusack! Can you *believe* that?"

"Yes Nathan, I can believe it. Who's going to play me, Mama Cass?"

"Aw come on babe," Nathan guffawed, "be serious, she's dead. No, they're going to have Nathan Steer—me—as single instead of married, so they can build up a romantic angle—every Hollywood story needs one—and give it a happier ending. What Waterman's thinking is that Nathan Steer—Matt Dillon or John Cusack—and Connie—Florence Henderson—will fall in love after Sal dies, and they'll get married and move back to Bakersfield! Pretty good, huh?"

"But Nathan, that isn't how it happened!

That isn't your book!"

"Aw Jules, they have to dramatize for the TV audience! And Abe says who knows where this could lead to, a dramatic series maybe? 'Peyton Place,' 'Dallas' and 'Knott's Landing' were all hits, 'La Sangre' could be too. It could go on and on, because the La Sangre story isn't over yet."

"It isn't?"

"Of course not Babe! Not by a long shot! Who knows what else will happen there by the time production starts on the mini-series?"

SIXTEEN

SANTA ROSA DISPATCH
September 16, 1985

WEDDING ANNOUNCEMENT

Theresa Virginia Spagopolous and Doyle Lucas Seeno will take their wedding vows on Saturday, September 20, at noon at the St. Constantine Greek Orthodox Church in Santa Rosa. Reception to follow.

Miss Spagopolous is of the family that owns Spago Brothers Greek Restaurant, and she is the founder of the Santa Rosa Greek Festival. Mr. Seeno is a mechanic for Emerald Ford in Santa Rosa and has lived in La Sangre for the past 11 years. The two met when Miss Spagopolous moved to La Sangre last June.

"Oh Theresa, giati mia to kanis auto!"

"I'm not doing *anything* to you, Mama! I'm just trying to live my life!"

"But Theresa," Papa matched Mama's tone, "you let us find this out in the paper? You don't tell us? You have aunts and uncles and cousins in Greece that might want to come over, just for your wedding! Iii monachocore mia! My only daughter!"

The three of them were sitting on the custom-made striped satin-covered couch—a possession of well-deserved pride for her Mama—in the Spagopolous' living room of their well-earned large Victorian style house in Healdsburg, north of Santa Rosa on US 101. That couch was where and how all family confrontations were held, sitting together, not in separate chairs looking at each other from afar. The receiver of this particular confrontation, Theresa, sat appropriately in between the two.

"Oh Papa I'm sorry," Theresa was near tears yet resolute. "I was sure you and Mama disapproved of him. You weren't very friendly when he was here."

"Well, iii omorfi kori mia, I shake his hand and he did not seem so sure. Your Mama go to kiss him and he was, uh how you say, stiff..."

"Oh Papa, he was just feeling a little uncertain, he's just not used to a roomful of screaming Greeks. It was the first time for him."

"Well," her Mama smirked, "he must get used to it if he wants to marry my beautiful daughter."

"He will Mama."

Mama was quiet for a few seconds, then asked tentatively "Koimithikes mazi the?"

"No Mama, I didn't sleep with him. We're waiting for our wedding night. I could tell he wanted to the first time we met, but I said no, I'm a good Greek Orthodox girl and will save myself for my husband." Theresa wasn't so sure that God was impressed with that vow one way or the other, but it made her parents happy, and being 29 years old and not having been with a man was no great sacrifice to her, certainly not based on the available shallow men people kept introducing her to.

"Well then," Papa began, "it's not too late to...."

Theresa turned to her Papa on the left. "No Papa, and that's telikos! Final!" She hugged him, then turned to the right and did the same for her Mama. It's what they did to signal the end of a Greek argument. "Papa, Mama, I know what I'm doing. I've been praying about it."

But Mama wasn't through, far from it. "But Theresa, he's an old man, he's twice your age!"

"Not *twice* my age, Mama, he's 50." That was a quibble; he was certainly old enough to be her father. "Besides Mama I'm all gray-haired. It evens out, he still has his dark Italian hair, and smooth skin!"

"Arrgh, Kyrios Seeno aux Italus," Papa waved dismissively.

"Stop it Papa! Cousin Urania married an Italian!"

"Aw that no good...."

"Skasse Papa!" Mama scolded him and turned back to Theresa. "But this Doyle, he's so tall, and skinny! Italian men are bigger, shorter, like the Greeks."

"Mama, I don't care about that. I love him, I *know* him!"

But Mama continued. "And all those handsome Greek men I tell you about, they are rich, they have restaurants in San Francisco, in San Jose..."

"And Theresa," Papa came back in, "this Doyle is just a mechanic. How much he make at Emerald Ford?"

"Papa, Doyle will get raises, even be promoted, I know he will. He's made his whole life all alone, with no family, no brothers and sisters like we have. Doyle made himself just like Pappous, your own Papa, did when he came here from Greece, sleeping in steerage. Pappous didn't know anything when he arrived at Ellis Island; he didn't speak English, he got on the train to San Francisco, and look what he did! Doyle is a self-made man, like Pappous. He's always worked hard, he's reliable and strong. You watch, he'll be a manager at Ford some day."

"At his age?"

"Yes, at his age. Please Mama, Papa, don't worry. It will all be right, all of it. Doyle will be in our family; he may not hug and kiss and scream like we do, but I will be his wife, and we will have your eggonia."

That made Mama and Papa quiet, until Papa spoke.

"They will be doctors," he decreed, "just like your nephew Demetrius."

"And if they're girls, Papa?"

He thought about it. "They will marry all those handsome rich Greek men your Mama always talk about."

Theresa smiled and leaned back in the comfortable couch and looked up at the sculpted ceiling, sweet surrender on her face. She was happy beyond words, though she still wondered how she could so love two people who could drive her crazy. She turned her head to the left.

"So, will you walk me down the aisle, Papa?"

The three Greeks burst into tears and managed a three-way embrace on the couch.

"Iii treli kori mia me to trelo charisma," Mama cried.

"Yes Mama," Theresa laughed through her tears, "I'm your crazy daughter, but Mama, Papa, that gift is waning since I met Doyle!"

"Waning?" Papa asked.

"Going away."

"Eucharist ton theo gia ta thaumata!" Papa cried out.

Yes, thank you God for miracles, Theresa silently, joyfully agreed.

The fall was surprisingly peaceful, at least by La Sangre standards. By Christmas of 1985, the town had become known as "The *New* La Sangre," and it marked California's first real mystical destination, just like Sedona, Arizona and Taos, New Mexico.

Only a couple of the longtime La Sangre residents remained, though they admitted that but for the location they'd rather live somewhere else. La Sangre was no longer united, with the church and its Pastor as the beacon. The four-foot chain link fence that was erected just weeks after Pastor Satori was killed looked stark and ugly at the edge of the bluff, a metaphor that the town had become a prison, full of dark people and, a few of the oldies believed, dark forces. Still, all was peaceful, to the eye anyway.

Most of the newcomers were polite, and they even came to church service, but they were ultimately disappointed with what they decided were the limited beliefs of the Bible. Such attitudes weren't really shocking so much as a reminder to the old-timers that there is still a sinful world out there, and they should be grateful that La Sangre was theirs alone for as long as it was. They can't own a town. After all, this was still the West; property owners come and go, and cities evolve around their lifestyles. Look at what happened to the saloon-and-whorehouse town of San Francisco in 1900. After World War

II, no working man could buy a home there.

One of the new La Sangre residents tried to talk to a couple of the originals about alternate routes to God, the power of the pyramid for example, and the healing it provides when placed under food and under the bed. The Pyramid Lady, as she became known behind her back, asked Corey if she could stock the General Store with pyramids, for sale on consignment.

Corey said he'd have to think about it and discuss it with his mother, who is now the owner of all the La Sangre businesses. Encouraged, Pyramid Lady reported this to a few others and, also encouraged, they had their own requests for new General Store items such as healing stones, ointments and herbs. Corey did think about it but he didn't share it with his mother, in his effort to keep the operation of the town away from her for now. But he knew that he was now the de facto head of the Satori Family, and had to make decisions, with regular counsel from Ralph and Matthew. Corey told the New Agers the herbs and ointments were fine, but he just wasn't comfortable selling the pyramids or healing stones. They politely agreed on that compromise.

Henry had to spend a month in Matthew's den (Matthew grinned and bore it) before Doyle moved out of the Garage and into Theresa's cottage after their wedding. Corey then generously repainted and re-carpeted the rooms, hall, stairs, and remodeled the bathroom. Henry moved in and used one room as his bedroom, and the other as his movie-watching room, with movie posters on the walls and a large screen TV, a housewarming gift from Matthew and Lillian. Matthew offered to pay rent for Henry but Corey told him no, appreciably and firmly; it's what his Father Sal would have done, just like he had done for Doyle.

But Henry was certainly no slouch. All day long he stood outside the Antique Store on the wooden walkway, wearing the cowboy garb that matched the Old West theme of the town, and waving and chatting with customers. He wore his cowboy hat well and fancied himself Ray Milland in "A Man Alone." Henry practically chain-smoked, but deftly flicked it into the spittoon when a potential customer approached.

Given his natural panache, whenever a customer entered the Antique Store, Henry managed to get a sale of some sort, and within two months his efforts had almost doubled the receipts. Encouraged, and with the Corey's appreciation and prudent expense, the store was revamped. Henry had his "The Birds" poster framed and placed in the front window; he correctly anticipated that most people would have driven north from Bodega Bay with that film in mind.

Most enterprisingly, Henry took his eight-by-ten glossy of Tippi Hedren in The Tides Restaurant to Santa Rosa Photo, and ordered a hundred post cards to sell at a dollar-per-postcard.

They sold out the first weekend. With the profits he ordered 500 more.

"You have permission to copy this likeness?" the clerk at Santa Rosa Photo asked Henry. The clerk hadn't asked him the first time, and knew he should have.

"Oh yeah I do," Henry lied effortlessly, "with Universal Studios!"

The clerk looked at him dubiously but took the order. That exchange told Henry he'd better not try to sell them bulk to The Tides Restaurant or anywhere else; but there was little chance anyone of importance from Universal would notice, or care, in such an out of the way place as the La Sangre Antique Store. So Henry kept those postcards on display inside the store and conscientiously reported the significant profits to Corey. Corey in return told Henry that in addition to his minimum pay, he could have meals gratis at the La Sangre Saloon, like they did for Doyle when he worked the Gas Station.

Henry's ideas kept coming. He borrowed a bucket from the Gas Station ("You make sure you bring this back," Micah said patronizingly, which Henry didn't notice.) and had Matthew drive him to Gleason Beach, four miles south of La Sangre, so he could gather rocks.

"Don't let Sheriff Daley catch you with that bucket of rocks," Matthew advised Henry as they drove back. "You know it's illegal along the California coast."

"Oh, it is? But Matthew, didn't I tell you what I was going to do with them?"

Did he? Matthew couldn't remember. His main responsibility was to drive Henry around when he had to, and invite him for occasional meals with him and Lillian; if Lillian had her way, Henry be there for every dinner. And per Lillian's order. Matthew took Henry to the dentist, and promised Lillian that he would spend time with Henry when he was in the mood to tolerate his brother's continual movie talk.

"Matthew," Henry interrupted his thoughts, "didn't I tell you what I was going to do with the rocks?"

"Oh, I guess I forgot, I'm sorry. What are you going to do with the rocks?" Matthew restrained himself from mimicking Henry's tone.

"Oh, well, I'm going to make a display in the store window, with these rocks in the antique gold mining pan that's in the store; and I'll have them sitting in water to keep them wet and shiny, with a sign that says 'Rocks From The Bloody La Sangre Cliffs - $2 each.' You know, kind of like the 'Pet Rocks' of...can't remember when, a while ago."

"1975," Matthew answered. "We gave them as the top prize at the game joints in the carnival. Guys would win them for their dates. Shoot, a guy would pay at least three times the cost of those things than if he just bought one in the store. More fun to win it at a carnival." Matthew, at that moment, could have called up West Coast Shows, found out where their nearest show was, not packed anything or left a note, gone out to the show, and get hired on as a roustabout. For at least a year.

Henry's cliff rocks sold out as quickly as the post cards, as many of them to the local La Sangre New Agers as to the tourists, the former of whom were certain there was indeed some mystical power from these La Sangre cliff rocks.

"Matthew, I'm thinking about sprinkling red paint over the next batch of rocks, you know, to look like blood!" Henry told him one night at dinner at his house.

Matthew winced and Lillian suppressed a smile.

"I think that might be pushing it," Lillian said gently.

Henry liked Lillian, and always listened to her. After all, she was his big brother's wife. "Yeah, I guess it would be like a William Castle movie."

"Who's that?" Matthew asked, and was immediately sorry he had.

"Oh wow, he's the producer and director who did movies like 'The Tingler' where the theater seats were wired to vibrate whenever the Tingler appeared, or 'House On Haunted Hill' where a skeleton burst out from a coffin next to the screen and flew out over the audience on a wire, or '13 Ghosts' where you use a mask when the ghosts appear on the screen so you can see them, and "Homicidal, where...."

"Oh yeah, I saw 'House On Haunted Hill.'" Matthew said. That was true, although he barely watched the film from the balcony seat that he practically shared with a young lady he met at the carnival. (Ooo! With his *wife* in the room?)

"They didn't do any of that extra William Castle stuff at The Grand," Henry went on, "or any theater in Topeka, but I was told the Midland Theater in Kansas City, Missouri did, so I took the bus there, and yeah, in 'House On Haunted Hill' that skeleton flew over our heads when Vincent Price was operating it to scare his wife. It was really cool!" He paused in joyous memory. "The Midland Theater is gone now, got torn down in '78."

Blessed silence for a few seconds.

"You know, William Castle produced 'Rosemary's Baby' too."

"Oh, that movie scared me," Lillian said.

She responded occasionally to give Henry some validation, though she wasn't so sure he really needed it.

"Yeah. I'll bet if William Castle was still alive, he'd make a movie about La Sangre. I wonder what his gimmick would be?"

"Maybe he'd make it a 3-D movie," Matthew quipped, "you know, to make you think you're actually falling off the cliff!"

"Hey!" Henry turned to him, surprised. "That's a pretty good idea, Matthew!"

"Thank you Henry!" Matthew was ready to play Henry's-A-Fool—he was in his carny mood—but Lillian shot him a look.

"I always wondered what your office looked like," Connie said to Ralph. It was indeed an office, soothing in browns and greens, with two relaxing pastoral oil paintings on the wall. There was a desk, and two comfortable-looking easy chairs. Dr. Ralph Owen, Psychiatrist, motioned Connie to one of the chairs.

"I mean," she sat down, "Sal spent a lot of time here, didn't he?"

"He did, or we'd sit out on the front porch." Ralph sat down. "You remember seeing Sal and me sitting on your deck, talking. You always brought us coffee."

"Oh," Connie hesitated, "yes, yes of course I remember that." She hadn't talked about her husband since the night he died. How long ago was that, three months?

She wasn't all there, Ralph saw. Breathing erratic and painful, eyes lacking clarity, voice overpitched.

"How are you getting on?" he asked her.

"I'm thinking about going back to Bakersfield," she responded, looking directly at him.

Ralph nodded. Good. That declaration focused herself. "Tell me about that."

Connie looked at him, her breathing decelerating. "That's all I know."

"And Connie, that's all you *need* to know, for now." Ralph considered it, and then took a gamble and breached the "religious line" psychiatrists are ordered not to cross. Too much of it and you could lose your license. Still he had to ask, "Have you been praying about it, Connie?"

Connie's eyes never left his. "I don't pray any more, Ralph, and I don't believe in God."

Every psychiatrist has at least one session that is carved into his soul, leaving a beautiful scar. That special session—this session—makes so many others feel mundane and routine by comparison. This one tested Ralph's integrity, his definition. And so far, he was blowing it as a shrink, because his face expressed, well, shock.

"Shocked?" Connie asked, not with hostility or judgment, she simply wanted to know.

Ralph leaned back in his seat and looked up at the ceiling. Yes, this was going to be one of *those* sessions. Here we go. "Connie, I'm not really equipped to...."

"Do it."

"What?" Ralph jerked his head from ceiling-gazing back to Connie.

"I need to know, I need proof, Ralph, one way or the other. My husband Sal was one of the strongest believers on Earth, and he told me you were an atheist. You two talked for hours! He considered you his best friend! What did you talk about? What did you two come up with? I need to know, so tell me. Is God real? Or is He dead?"

By this time it wasn't about losing his license, it wasn't even about Connie so much as about himself. He was in a lose/lose/lose situation. If he answered "Yes" he'd be a liar. If he answered "No" it could destroy this very hurting—however innately strong, he still believed—woman, and for what? His Hippocratic Oath? And if he answered "I don't know," he'd be letting Connie, his client, down, something he'd never done in his life. Clients may have left *him*, but he never left them, even when it came to money they didn't have.

"Is God real?" Connie repeated, softly and determined. "Or is God dead?"

"Connie, how could I prove any answer I may give?"

Connie considered it. Fair question, actually a very good one. "Sal told me that he often prayed with you. Is that true?"

Ralph nodded.

"Then I'd like to see you pray now, Ralph. You either will or you won't, you can say what you want, or do nothing at all. You can even be silent about it. Just do it, or not. I need proof."

Ralph was frozen at the pitcher's mound. Connie saw it. "Ralph, let me tell you something Sal told me when I first met him, and maybe he told you this too. We're not to use prayer like a vending machine, putting a coin in the slot and removing our choice of candy. We're to pray for attributes, not things."

"Attributes? Like what?"

"Patience, wisdom, forgiveness, peace, strength. You pray for those things and you always get them, and after that everything just works out. Most often we see it happen in finances, where it always works out. So Ralph, just say what's in your heart, about what you think I need, what you'd like to see for me, what our next step in therapy will be. Say it to God, out loud, from your heart." She smiled, and then added, not without humor, "If He's there."

Private First Class Ralph Owen was a Marine Paratrooper over Germany in World War II. This would be his last jump.

He jumped from the plane, the static line

took, and Ralph was never the same.

Doyle sat at the kitchen table, still in his work coveralls, and watched Theresa stir the pot on the stove. Garlic and basil filled the air, she had her glass of Greek Nemea red wine within reach, while Doyle had a bottle of Lone Star Beer in front of him. It was a nonstop amusement of theirs, where she'd playfully yell at him in Greek ("You go to Sonoma County's most expensive liquor store just to get your lousy old Texas beer, and then you have the *audacity* to drink it with my cooking, the best Greek food in Sonoma County! Mama and Papa were right about you!") and Doyle would just grin and take a slurp of his beer, wiping his mouth with the back of his hand.

"So what did you do today?" Doyle asked Theresa.

"Well, I formally met Stellar Sky," she said.

"Stella Who?"

"*Stellar* Sky. The Pyramid Lady. It's the first time we really spoke besides a friendly hello."

"'Stellar Sky,'" Doyle repeated. "Is that her real name?"

"Oh, about as real as 'Madame Athena.'"

Doyle chuckled. "So what'd she have to say?"

"Well, she explained to me the power of moonlight, especially a full moon, when she takes a moon bath. She gets some kind of power from the full moon, but it's too cold here at night to go out in her one-piece swimming suit. She said for the next full moon she'll go to a friend's home in Santa Rosa and moon-bathe in her back yard."

"Well, that's good, I guess." He got up and went to the stove, putting his arms around Theresa's waist from behind. "I want to tell you something."

"Yes?" She knew what it was, and not because of her gift, which in their two-month marriage was almost completely distinguished. She reached for the oregano leaves and crumbled a little into the bubbling Greek tomato sauce, without interrupting Doyle's hold.

"I like myself ever since we've met," Doyle told her. "I love you, that part's obvious, but I love...I love who I am. Who you made me to be."

She stopped stirring and turned around, putting her arms around his neck.

"You did that yourself, darling, I just sort of...revved up the engine."

"You can say that again," he gave her a strong kiss.

She smiled. "I'm going to tell you what my Yaya told me..."

"Oh your Yaya again..."

"Yes, my Yaya again. Since I was a little girl, she'd tell me 'To nha eisai alithini gynaika einai nha bgazeis to kalytero so enan andhra."

Doyle frowned. "All I got out of that was 'woman' and 'man.'"

"See? You're getting better! It means 'To be a real woman is to bring out the best in a man.'"

"Hey," Doyle pulled his head back, truly surprised. "Won't that kind of talk get you in trouble with 'the movement?'"

"Oh I know, isn't it awful? But in my readings to women, to help me see where they're coming from, I often ask 'Would you be happy just taking care of and pleasing a man?'"

"That's a politically charged question."

"Tell me about it. But a lot of them, instead of just answering 'Yes' or 'No, that wouldn't be enough for me,' they go ballistic, like how dare I ask such a degrading question! They've lost their sense of humor." Theresa shrugged and went back to her sauce. "Most of them were abused by some man, I used to get those visions, but I don't always tell them, because instead of forgiving the man who abused them, they already politicized their anger, and now they have a platform of revenge they live on, and all the angry-women-enablement they want. And yet they keep coming back to me and I ask them the same thing, and then I ask them to consider their violent reaction. Eventually some don't go so crazy and start looking at themselves, at what their anger is about."

"You sound like Dr. Owen."

Theresa nodded. “I guess I’m just a shrink who has visions.”

“Like you had of me.”

Theresa stopped stirring the pot and turned back to him. “Yes, and I saw a beautiful man, a powerful man, that’s what I saw. It’s the greatest vision I ever had as Madame Athena. And the last vision.”

Beautiful, full silence.

“Theresa....” was all Doyle could manage.

Theresa turned back to the stove, and lowered the burner to simmer.

An hour later they were holding each other, listening to the ocean outside the bedroom window.

“Doyle, I was going to tell you this after dinner, but I think I’ll tell you now.”

“Say it in Greek, see if I can figure it out. I think I’m getting better.”

“Okay. Eimai egypos.”

“Hmm. And you were going to tell me this after dinner?”

“Nai.”

“‘Yes.’ Okay, let’s see....you were going to say ‘Do you want some coffee, Hon?’”

“Oxy!”

“‘No?’ Okay, I give up.”

“Well in English and a longer version,” Theresa took his face in her hands, “I haven’t gotten my period since our wedding night. I went to the doctor yesterday to make sure, and he called me today and said 'Yes.'"

Doyle raised himself on his elbow. "Theresa?"

She nodded, still smiling. "Nai!"

He lay back down and pulled her close. "You did this for me?"

"For both of us."

"I'm...I'm the happiest...and the oldest...father in the world!"

"The *best* father in the world. Just like you're the best husband."

He knew he would be the former, and he already knew he was the latter. "But tell me Terri, before you went to the doctor, did you have a vision about it, or a dream, like of a stork or something?"

"Oh you silly! I told you I stopped having those visions so often after we met, and almost totally after we got married. I'm not Madame Athena anymore, I don't care, and I don't miss it."

"Really? But you're still seeing people, giving them readings."

"If you want to call it that," Theresa chuckled. "I'm just on autopilot, getting the same questions and giving the same answers. I just use the same common sense that an advice columnist uses. I don't need visions for that. Actually, I feel like telling them all to just get a life." She lay her head on Doyle's slim, hairless chest, firmed up from eight to ten hours a day at Emerald Ford, often six days a week. "No, even though I guess I'm helping them, I feel like I'm cheating them because they're not getting anything mystical, no hocus-pocus, what they paid for." She sighed. "I'm going to hang up my Madame Athena turban and just be a wife and a mother. But," she pulled back and looked him in the eyes. "wait until you hear what the delivery date of our baby is."

"When?"

"June 15."

"Oh no, you don't mean...."

"Yes. Father's Day."

They looked at each other for a moment, not knowing what to do with it at first. Then they burst into laughter.

Since Theresa had first arrived in La Sangre home, she wanted to have a conversation with Dr. Owen. She got a solid, intelligent vibe from him. After the wedding ceremony he had sincerely and properly kissed her and thanked her for making Doyle so happy. They'd nod and smile whenever they'd see each other, but he always kept a distance. Theresa was sure that the good doctor was respecting her space with Doyle, whom she knew he had been treating for over a year, and that Doyle had "graduated."

But Theresa had some questions for Dr. Owen about herself, and she saw an opportunity when she was driving down the road to the homes; he was standing at the cliff fence, watching the ocean. She parked and walked out to him.

Ralph heard the grass swishing behind him and turned around. Theresa was walking towards him, and he knew their time to talk had arrived. He was glad. They greeted each other.

"I'd like to talk to you, if I may," Theresa smiled sheepishly, for her anyway. "I've been wanting to."

Ralph nodded. It wouldn't serve well to tell her that he was aware of that.

"It's about me," she explained, "not my husband. Would that be a conflict?"

"No, as long as we stick with just you."

"How much do you charge?"

"For Mrs. Doyle Seeno, nothing."

"Really? We could have done a trade. I make good money—or *used* to make good money—uh, doing readings."

"Yes 'Madame Athena,'" Ralph smiled.

"Wow, word sure gets around quickly in La Sangre!"

"Well, small town, you know. But what can I do for you?"

"Well, maybe I just need to know if I'm, well, 'normal.'"

"Oh yeah, *that* word, 'normal.' As in, does your life experience fall within a continually narrowing acceptable segment of the human population?"

"Well, I can't say I need approval, I'm just trying to understand something. My gift for sight, for visions, never scared me as a child. It made my family uncomfortable but they learned to live with it. I didn't abuse my gift, even when I started charging for it as 'Madame Athena.'"

"I'm sure you didn't."

"And now it's gone and I'm relieved. I lost it when Doyle and I met and married, I might have an occasional vision after the wedding, but now that I'm three months pregnant, it's gone for good, and I'm glad. I'm just curious Doctor...."

"Ralph."

"Ralph. Is that what happens to such gifts, when you get married? I mean, it sounds like one of those Greek myths my Yaya would tell me at bedtime. When a god or goddess falls in love with a mortal, he or she loses their gift, as well as their place on Mt. Olympus with Zeus and the other gods. I'm curious, Ralph, what is your opinion, as a psychiatrist, about all this, what I call a 'gift?'"

Ralph was relieved. She was indeed just talking about herself, there'd be no breach of confidence. "Well first of all, your Yaya wasn't wrong. Classically, when an innocent young girl had visions, say like Joan of Arc, she was considered pure and touched by God. Of course in America it was considered the work of the devil."

"Like the Salem witch hunts?"

"Right. But after Freud arrived in the 20th Century, the virgin with visions became characterized as repressed and hysterical, and any such visions or prophecies were considered the product of an unhealthy, unfulfilled spirit, or soul."

"So I met and fell in love with Doyle—and I'm still not sure what or if La Sangre's strange aura had anything to do with it—and after our wedding night, the gift disappeared."

Ralph nodded and smiled, more for himself. He had long wondered if and when he'd be able to refer to the only patient of his, about twenty years ago, who had a gift of foresight.

"I've experienced that before," Ralph said.

Theresa looked at him. "You? A psychiatrist? You mean you feel the strange aura here?"

"No!" Ralph laughed. "Certainly not me! I'm not an aura kind of guy."

"Oh, I guess I was being silly."

"No, not at all. Actually it was a patient of mine, quite a while ago. In her growth she got to where she could accept the visions and and not let them bother her, as you were able to do."

"Did her gift go away after she got married? Got pregnant?"

"I don't know," Ralph shook his head. "She still had it when I was seeing her, and I haven't heard from her since." Ralph studied Theresa, such a beautiful young woman, from whom joy radiated. "I know you know that Doyle still sees me occasionally, and forgive me this minor breach, but he told me what you said to him when you two first met, that Nothing Matters."

Theresa nodded and smiled at Ralph, and turned to the ocean. Ralph followed her gaze. Their session was over.

Crazy town or not, crazy people or not, sinners all, the Pacific Ocean reigned, a miracle of sight, smell, sound and occasional fury.

And Nothing Mattered. until....

SUNDAY, JUNE 15, 1986
FATHER'S DAY

SEVENTEEN

At 5:30 AM on Father's Day morning, Jay and Barnabas met Phil Stevens in The Tides parking lot. The morning fog was unusually heavy, the sun still below the horizon.

"You're sure you can drive me up to La Sangre and be back in time for your six o'clock opening?" Jay asked him. "It's pretty foggy."

"Yeah, more fog than usual." He led Jay through the parking lot. "Kinda strange. But no, I can get you up there and back in time." He stopped at a truck in the last aisle.

"Nice Dodge, Phil."

"Yeah, it's an '83, good shape though."

"Sure is. You want Barney to ride in the back?"

"Naw, Barnabas rides with us, it's an extended cab." He opened the right rear door. "Hop in Barney!"

They had a slow, comfortably silent ride through the fog until they reached Gleason Beach, where the traffic suddenly stopped.

"Oh no," Phil moaned, "they're already lined

up to gawk, thinking something's going to happen again just cause it's Father's Day, as if anything will really happen three times in a row. Yeah right. Well Jay," he turned to the passenger seat, "do you think we...."

The passenger seat was empty. Phil looked in the rear seat, Barnabas was gone.

Phil shrugged it off and made a hand signal to the car coming up behind him that he was pulling a U-turn, a challenge for a full-sized Dodge pickup on the narrow Highway One, in heavy fog no less. But he made a clean three-point U-turn and headed south.

"Well, saved me waiting in that line to La Sangre," Phil said to himself. The Tides opened in fifteen minutes; he'll be on time, easy, even with the fog.

"Just another day," Phil said to himself gratefully. "Doesn't make much difference."

It was still dark when Henry woke up, having fallen asleep in the recliner in his movie room, After closing the Antique Store at 6 PM and having dinner at Matthew and Lillian's, he treated himself to a 1950s sci-fi triple feature at home. First up was 1955's "Day The World Ended," then the original 1956 version of "Invasion Of The Body Snatchers." Somehow both of them deeply disturbed him, though he'd seen them dozens of times and knew them by heart. But this time in

"Body Snatchers," Kevin McCarthy's apocalyptic warning of "YOU'RE NEXT! YOU'RE NEXT!" unnerved Henry, as if he was actually, finally, understanding what it meant for him.

He should have stopped there and gone in to bed, but his desire for some kind of truth made him proceed with the third film, 1957's "The Incredible Shrinking Man." But he fell asleep shortly after the beginning, because it too was hitting him hard, like the first two films did, even though he also knew "Shrinking Man" by heart. But why, after 30 years of seeing these films over and over, ever since The Grand Theater, did these three films finally, especially the last one, frighten him so? That was the last concrete thought he had before willing himself to sleep, something he became adept at after his father left.

In anticipation of an early morning lineup of cars with people hoping to see a third murder and/or suicide in La Sangre, starting on Saturday afternoon deputies were stationed at the north and south ends of La Sangre. This was more than for just controlling the relatively harmless rubberneckers, there were plenty of morbid, horror-obsessed people who were ready to unleash their frustrations on that town; murder and suicide weren't far beyond their sphere of behavior. And the unusually heavy fog was an enabling veil for anyone's uncontrolled, misdirected passion.

The cliff naturally protected La Sangre from the west, Highway One was blocked north and south, and deputies roamed the grazing hills east of town, in case the most determined fans of the mini-series tried sneaking over the coastal hills into their Xanadu.

Henry sat in his recliner, fully awake now, still reeling from his triple-horror binge. "The Incredible Shrinking Man" was long over, the digital clock on the Beta machine read 5:45 AM. The fog was so thick it seemed to be seeping through the thin, single-pane windows of the room.

Still fully dressed, he got up and went to the bathroom. He then went into his bedroom and put on his shoes, unsure what he was going to do.

You're the incredible shrinking man, Henry.

Yes. I am.

He put on a jacket and went down the stairs and outside, standing next to the gas pumps. The sun was making a valiant effort to rise above the horizon against the thick fog. Henry looked across the One to the chain link fence along the cliff. Why was the fence and ocean so clear, given all the fog surrounding the town?

He saw why: the Pacific Ocean was

neatly parted in the middle just like in "The Ten Commandments," when Charlton Heston stretched out his arms and staff and the Red Sea parted so he could lead God's people out of Egypt to freedom.

But no, it wasn't the ocean that had parted, it was the fog, creating walls on either side, so that if he walked through those walls of fog it would be like....

"Like 'The Incredible Shrinking Man!'" Henry said aloud. In "Shrinking Man" Grant Williams was on the bow of his boat while it was adrift in the ocean, when a weird mist from the horizon approached. The mist hit Williams and left a painless sparkly residue on his skin, and after that he began gradually shrinking. The doctors and scientists did everything they could to stop it, to get Grant Williams back to normal size, but he just kept on shrinking.

Henry and Matthew's mother, Daisy Grant, died in 1957 right after "Shrinking Man" was released. The first time Henry saw it, the day it opened, he knew he had found his place in the universe. He watched every single screening of the film at The Grand, in between cleaning the seats, and after the film left Topeka, he rented it and watched it over and over, alone in the empty theater, from the midnight closing to the theater's opening the next day at noon. Over and over he watched it.

Henry had found his home.

And now, like a gift from God, Henry saw the pathway to home in the ocean. It wasn't exactly the mist like in the movie, but rather an opening in the fog, inviting him, ready to envelope and comfort him, to make him feel safe and loved. Once surrounded by the fog, Henry would then slowly shrink away, to where he was no larger than a pixel on the movie screen. Millions would watch his beloved movies, but no one could see him, as he lived happily within the celluloid. It was a place where Henry belonged, where he would be an integral and eternal part of the beautiful alternate reality of the movies.

Though the deputies weren't far from where Henry was standing at the gas station, they couldn't see or hear him as he walked across Highway One and headed toward the ocean.

He climbed over the fence, unafraid as he neared the love and acceptance that God was offering him. He was sure he could actually hear God calling him.

He took seven steps beyond the fence.

He was almost home.

The ground beneath Henry gave way and he fell to the bottom of the cliff.

EIGHTEEN

At the moment Henry hit the bottom, a fishing boat owned by a Greek American fisherman, Constantine Spagopolous, and his teenage son Demetrius, emerged from the southern wall of fog.

"Papa!" Demetrius pointed. Just a quarter mile ahead of them a second solid wall of fog stood, parallel to the one behind them.

"I see Deme! I know!"

"Papa!" Demetrius cried again, this time pointing eastward. The two fog walls ended on the shore, marking the northern and southern borders of....

"La Sangre, Papa!" Demetrius cried.

"Cross yourself Deme! Do not even say the name of that town! Do not look at it Deme! Put those binoculars down and cross yourself!"

Deme crossed himself but didn't lower the binoculars. "But Papa look!" he pointed. "The cliff! Below!"

Gus lifted his own binoculars and gasped. "No! It cannot be!"

At the bottom of the cliff a body lay among the rocks.

"Oh no!" Gus cried out. "I can not tell, Deme, is it a man or a woman? Your Aunt Theresa, she lives in La Sangre! Her baby is due today!"

"I don't know, Papa, I can't tell!"

"We call the Costa Guard, now!"

The large chunk of ground that gave way under Henry actually served as a dirty protectant as he slid down the 70 foot cliff face, and as a cushion upon which he landed at the bottom. Still, he heard and felt both his hips snap.

He sat on the bottom, among the rocks. The tide had ebbed enough for the salt water to wet Henry just up to the waist; the freezing cold water would create a natural anesthetic for the pain, after the protection of shock wore off.

"Well Henry Grant, that was just about the dumbest thing you've ever done," said a voice next to him.

Henry looked over to the right. "It sure was!" He recognized Jay. "Hey, I know you!"

"Of course you do."

"In 'Ben-Hur,' when Charlton Heston is dying of thirst, and the centurion said 'No water for him!' But you stood up to the guard and after he backed down, you knelt and poured the wooden ladle of water onto your hand, you let it spill on Heston's face, you wiped the water on his forehead, and touched his fingers. Then you raised his head and he drank, while you held the ladle, and you ran your fingers through his hair." Henry looked at him. "But we never got to see your face. You're handsome."

Jay shrugged. "It depends upon the artist. Wait until you see Willem Dafoe play me in 'The Last Temptation Of Christ' in two years. It's already in production."

"William Dafoe? He was in 'Platoon.' He's ugly."

"Maybe so," Jay chuckled. "but he's a good actor. And Martin Scorcese is signed to direct..."

"Wow, he directed 'Taxi Driver' and 'Raging Bull!'"

"...so between Scorcese and Dafoe, they come the closest to showing the real me." Jay gave a deep sigh. "Now, as far as your going over that fence and standing at the edge of the cliff, do you remember why Deborah Kerr got hit by that car in 'An Affair To Remember?'"

"Sure. Because she was looking up at the Empire State Building, where she was to meet Cary Grant, and she didn't see the car coming."

"And what did she tell Grant, at the end of the movie?"

Henry fast-forwarded to the end. "She said to Cary Grant, 'I was looking up. It was the nearest thing to heaven. You were there.'"

Jay grinned and nodded. "We always like

to look up to heaven. But we have to be careful down here on Earth, watch our step, what we do and say. I've told everyone to be 'as harmless as a dove but wary as a serpent.'"

"Oh, yeah, I guess I haven't been so good on the second part. But what was that big tunnel, that wall of fog?"

"That was just my Father doing what people call a freak of nature. High pressure, low pressure. He was trying to communicate with you, but Henry, that fence is there for a reason. Anyway, the fog tunnel allowed two fishermen to see you, they just called 9-1-1."

"Oh, I guess I put God to a foolish test, like James Stewart in 'It's A Wonderful Life.'" Henry looked around at the rocks and sea. "So, am I dead? Did I go to hell?"

"No to both."

"Oh, well, I guess that's good. But the pain is starting now in my hips, my legs, even in the freezing water. How will we get out of here?"

"Just take my hand."

The people of La Sangre had no idea anything had happened until they were wakened by the sirens of the ambulance, the paramedics, and the firefighters with their well-equipped rescue vehicle.

Matthew and Lillian dressed in a rush and ran out to the cliff. The other few original townspeople, including Connie, Corey, Ralph, Julie, Doyle and Theresa, were truly horrified. Nathan Steer and Anne Owen, now successful authors, felt they'd received a gift from heaven, and they prepared for their TV interviews. And the self-proclaimed Enlightened Ones relished what the SAA boys called the Cosmic Orgasm. "Oh yes! It's happening again! It's Father's Day! Orion has descended!"

One of the firefighters was on his stomach, aiming his spotlight over the ledge. "HEY!" he shouted to the body, probably in vain but it's what they did; assume nothing.

Henry managed a feeble "Hey" but Jay shouted back for him.

"HEY! IT'S ME! HENRY GRANT!"

Matthew heard it from behind the chain link fence and shouted "HENRY!" On pure adrenaline he leaped over the fence.

"NO, SIR! NO!" a paramedic grabbed Matthew around the waist to keep him from running to the edge. The last thing they needed was a second body down there..

"BUT HE'S MY *BROTHER*!" Matthew screamed, writhing. Lillian stood by in helpless tears, praying out loud.

"All right man," the paramedic told Matthew. "We'll crawl to the edge, next to David out there, see him? He said there's a fresh break in the ground, and it might extend, so crawl *slowly*! Now come on." They got down and slid like earthworms to the edge, on either side of David, whose spotlight was on Henry, half-sitting in the rocks.

Matthew reached David's right side, the paramedic on his left. "David," the paramedic said, "this is the victim's brother."

David put his arm around Matthew's shoulders to secure him. "Go ahead," David said, "call him."

"HENRY, IT'S ME MATTHEW! HOLD ON! THEY'RE GOING TO BRING YOU OUT!"

"MATTHEW!" Jay shouted back. "HELP ME!"

"Well he's conscious, and his strength is good," David said to Matthew and the other paramedic, "if he can yell like that over the ocean. Larry, crawl back and tell the guys what we have to do. It looks like they're backing up over the fence and readying the winch. And you...?"

"Matthew."

"...Matthew, you just *stay still*! Keep talking to your brother, but *don't move!*"

The rescue truck backed up, flattening the chain link fence and going as far to the edge as they deemed safe. Two rescuers from the truck quickly repelled down the cliff, and a stretcher was lowered by the truck's crane. The two repellers talked to Henry and assessed his injuries, then gently and expertly placed him in the stretcher, which was carefully hoisted to the top. Matthew crawled back and saw the stretcher holding his little brother pass overhead and lowered next to the ambulance. Matthew had to be restrained, again, as he almost jumped onto the stretcher to be with Henry.

"Matthew!" Henry cried with whatever energy he had, reaching out for him. "You came to get me!"

Theresa, a full nine months pregnant, stood with an attentive Doyle and Lillian. "Doyle, Lillian, my water just broke." She and Doyle had planned to get a hotel room near the hospital today in case the road to Santa Rosa was clogged with gawkers.

"Are you...all right?" Doyle asked, almost in a panic. They should have taken the hotel room last night.

"It's all right Doyle," Lillian told him. "I've done this many times." She asked Theresa the usual questions about pains and dilations.

"I'll get the car," Doyle said. That at least was something he could do.

"No," Lillian said, "I have a better idea." A second ambulance had arrived, in case a second body had to be retrieved, and Lillian recognized one of the paramedics. "I'll be right back," she told Theresa and Doyle.

"Henry," Matthew managed to keep hold of Henry's hand as his stretcher was unhooked from the rescue truck and transferred into the ambulance. "I'll never leave you. I'll stay with you. Always."

"Can..." Henry asked one of the paramedics, "can my brother ride in the ambulance with me?"

"Sure he can!" she responded. "I'll be in there too, checking your vitals, and I'll give you something for the pain. Henry, it looks like you're going to be all right."

"Did..." Matthew was choking on his tears, "...did you hear that, Henry? I'm going to ride with you, and you're going to be all right! Did you hear her?"

"Matthew...yes, I heard her. As long as you don't leave me, I can be happy for the rest of my life. Just like Abbott and Costello! Remember how we saw them at The Grand Theater? In person?"

"I remember," Matthew sobbed. "Yes. We'll be just like Abbott and Costello."

Connie was watching the turmoil from her deck—as close as she wanted to get—with Corey beside her, holding Freeman, who didn't seem at all bothered by all the noise and shouting. Ralph was standing next to them. Like everyone else he awoke to the sirens, but Anne told him she needed time make herself up, knowing the news media would soon arrive. She told Ralph, "Now you pay careful attention to everything that goes on so I can get the details for an update to my book." Ralph firmly replied, "If you're going to call yourself a journalist, you forget the makeup and go see for yourself," and he left the house. When he saw the Satoris on their deck, he joined them, ever vigilant of Connie.

Julie stood watching Nathan being interviewed live by ABC's Sandra Billings. Julie was truly happy for him, and she knew that their marriage was over.

Lillian and Doyle carefully walked Theresa over to the ambulance, where Theresa was loaded up onto the stretcher, Doyle jumping in after her, and siren blasting, off they went to Santa Rosa General Hospital.

The other ambulance followed them. Within, Matthew sat next to his brother, his left hand on Henry's hands clasped over his chest, his right hand running through Henry's trimmed brown hair, with its recent touches of gray.

"I love you Matthew."

"I love you Henry."
"Forever and ever?"
"Forever and ever."

JULY 1, 1986 - JUNE 13, 1987

NINETEEN

Enough was enough, as far as the State of California was concerned.

The California Geological Survey, under the California Department of Conservation, officially announced:

> The bluff on which La Sangre sits is a geological time bomb, which could be catastrophic for human habitation. An earthquake of 6.0 on the Richter Scale or less could cause, at most, slight damage to modern construction, but could cause major damage to poorly constructed buildings, such as at La Sangre.

The California Department of Transportation quickly followed with:

> While we appreciate La Sangre's charm as a much loved stop on the drive up and down Highway One, we have determined that the necessary improvement of safety on Highway One between Bodega Bay and Jenner requires the removal of La Sangre.

Sonoma County agreed:

> The removal of La Sangre, while sad, is necessary to the improvement and safety of the infrastructure of Sonoma County and California.

The Governor of California signed the bill quickly, issuing his statement to the press:

> The tragedies over the last two years are not in any way a part of the decision to dismantle the lovely town of La Sangre. The small coastal town is an important part of California history, but it is no longer deemed safe for human habitation, particularly regarding potential and likely earthquakes. Property owners will be reimbursed for the current market value of their homes as of June 15, 1986, and I must stress that the latest incident in La Sangre, on June 15, 1986, regarding Henry Grant, was ruled an accident by the Sonoma County Sheriff Department.
>
> We regret this has to be done, and we will all miss going through and stopping at La Sangre on our drives up and down the most scenic coastal route in America. To that end, the new La Sangre Vista Point will be a beautiful addition to Highway One, offering spectacular views and restroom facilities.

Californians—indeed the nation—was left with nothing but questions. Further, they bemoaned the loss of what may have been a magic place, for good or for evil. Nobody believed the

Sheriff Department's inquest verdict that the Henry Grant incident was an accident. It was a botched suicide, everyone was certain of that. They all knew that it was La Sangre's dark forces, whatever they were, that drove him to suicide.

California's Restitution and Relocation of the La Sangre residents was cheap compared to the tens of millions usually spent in R&R on new roadways throughout the state, which sometimes wiped out complete urban neighborhoods, and cut farmlands in half. In the case of La Sangre, there were 25 homes, six of which were owned and rented out by the Satoris, now going for an average of $350,000, along with the five businesses owned by the Satori Family, which netted them a couple million.

Most of the town, including, and refreshingly many of the New Agers, spent practically every evening in the La Sangre Christian Church, discussing and praying about what they'll all do. Gratefully, a spirit of sad acceptance was reached in the tiny church, and a date was chosen for a joint yard sale for the residents, who were certain that people would pay top dollar for a worn-out easy chair "that once was in a home in *La Sangre*!" And they weren't wrong. After all, those saggy old cushions must have absorbed a lot of "La Sang-Rays," the term was born.

A separate day was chosen for a public

auction of the businesses and the church. A new Santa Rosa restaurant paid $55,000 for the church's four antique stained glass windows and the antique organ. All Corey wanted from the church was the white cross on the steeple.

The ABC-TV Mini-Series, "The Secret of La Sangre," based on Nathan Steer's book, was aired in April, 1987. It received record-breaking Nielsen Ratings—even against "Growing Pains" and "Who's The Boss?"—and uniformly bad reviews, most of which cited the horrible casting and over-the-top melodrama. The Jay Carpenter character, that Nathan had treated in his book as...

> ...an auto-induced wishful Christian apparition, charged by intense loneliness and the need to see their idea of some godly individual in solid, physical form, not unlike fans of science fiction/fantasy books and movies.
>
> The first alleged sighting and mention of the angelic apparition was from San Francisco 49er Peter Freeman, when he arrived in La Sangre on Saturday, June 16, 1984. Freeman's description of the supposed angelic hitchhiker who used to be a cop ran through the town, until many La Sangre residents became convinced that they too saw the apparition that Freeman named 'Jay Carpenter.' (Get it?) Some of these witnesses included

> well-educated people like Registered Nurse Lillian Walker Grant and Psychiatrist Dr. Ralph Owen.
>
> The whole thing was just a subconscious modern day replay of the French legend of Bernadette, who in 1858 claimed she saw a beautiful woman in the town dumps, and the villagers were convinced that what the girl saw was the the Blessed Virgin Mary. It's a contagion of loneliness and self-deception wherein a sense of satisfaction and peace is achieved in exchange for an endless suspension of the susceptible viewer's own reality.

...was changed by the writers and producers of the mini-series into some kind of Fairy Godmother who grants everyone's wish. And as promised, the whole affair was given a happy ending, with Nathan and Connie holding hands at the cliff, watching the sun set.

The old La Sangre residents—most of whom were now scattered around Sonoma County—watched the mini-series and asked themselves and each other, "Is that supposed to be *us*?" Their friends, co-workers. and the congregations at their new churches asked them, "Was that supposed to be *you*?"

Corey asked Dr. Owen, "Can we sue ABC-TV for making us all look like idiots?"

They were standing by the new six-foot-high

chain link fence, that was erected the day after Father's Day. If anyone felt imprisoned by the four-foot fence, this one cinched it.

"We could," Ralph shrugged, "but we'd have to prove damages, besides just embarrassing us."

"Damages?"

"Were we refused a job, or fired from a job, because of how we were portrayed on some silly TV show? Have we been harassed, any more so than just living here with the gawkers driving through? Corey, the public will have forgotten about that ridiculous show by next week. It's not worth the aggravation and cost of filing a lawsuit. Besides, they changed our names, those studio lawyers have it all sewn up."

"Oh right, big change. I was 'Carl Scarinci.'"

Ralph laughed. "Well at least they made some unveiled attempt at changing our names. Our friend Nathan Steer sure didn't."

"So...could *he* be sued?"

"Sure, you can sue anybody, but I'll say the same as for the TV show, it's not worth it. It'll just attract more attention to ourselves. Like *Valley Of The Dolls*. The more people complained about how crass it was, the more copies it sold, and then it was made into a silly movie..."

"Never heard of it."

"See what I mean? But the publishers claimed it sold more copies than the Bible. I'm sure it did." Ralph grabbed the galvanized webbing of the chain link fence and looked out at the ocean. "Anne recorded that stupid *Secret Of La Sangre* show and plays the Beta tape almost daily, like eating junk food. I have to leave the house when it's on. She's watching it now, with her coffee and toast."

Within this new, relaxed connection, Corey realized for the first time there was a part of his father, Sal, in Ralph. And Ralph was in Sal, as the two—so his mother told him—had spent hours together on Ralph's porch or the Satoris' deck, just talking. Sometimes they helped each other with chores, at their homes or at the church. They often rode into town together to Santa Rosa Hardware.

"Hey, uh, Dr. Owen," Corey said, following Ralph's gaze to the sea, "thanks for being such a good friend to my Dad."

"You're very welcome Corey. It was my pleasure. And by the way, it's 'Ralph.'"

Nathan got a call from his agent the day after the fourth and final episode of ABC's "The Secret Of La Sangre," telling him his current publisher is offering a $150,000 advance if he'll write another book, to be titled *The Death of La Sangre.* ("We'll have no problem getting another contract with ABC for a second mini-series, based on that title alone! I just hope all the original cast will be available.") All of this, along with an overloaded schedule of book signings, college lectures, and radio, TV and print interviews, made Nathan Steer a very rich young man.

Julie Johnson Steer got on with her new single life with a passion. She dusted off a dream she'd had since she was 14 and enrolled in medical school at University of California, San Francisco. She lived in the dorm, signed up for an excruciating body fitness program, and devoured her classes. She wanted nothing from her ex-husband, including his name.

Charley Johnson, Julie's father, was a misplaced Californian from Nebraska. He couldn't deny California's diverse beauty, but he quickly determined that people who will just look you in the eye and tell you what's what were a rarity, not the norm. When Julie brought Nathan Steer home for the first time, Charley knew Nathan was the California norm. But to see his admittedly plain-Jane, large-hipped beautiful-to-him daughter so happy, there was nothing he could do or say. Helen didn't have to nudge him. He kept his mouth shut even through the divorce.

Surprisingly Charley wasn't surprised when Nathan stopped by some time after Julie went off to medical school. Nathan gave Charley a very large check, telling him that he just wants Julie to have it, and is there any way that Julie won't know it came from him?

Words came easily with Charley Johnson. "Well thank you, Nathan. Yes, I'll accept it for her, and I'm sure we all appreciate it. It'll go straight into her medical schooling. We'll let her assume it's coming from us, but in our estate we'll tell her that it came from you, and let her figure out what she wants to do with that information."

With the money Ruby made on her La Sangre home, and with the freedom of not having to share it with her estranged sister, she bought a small, utterly charming beach cottage in Eureka. True to her promise to God, she did volunteer work for and within the St. Francis Abbey. With Mother Superior's misgivings, Ruby signed on as a postulant but, loving her new home and life in Eureka as she did, she just couldn't proceed with taking the vows. The long hours of Holy Silence drove her nuts; she enjoyed talking to anyone who would listen, 24/7. And poverty just wasn't her style. The outings that Mother Superior told her about were far too seldom. And so, good old Ruby Rogers was back. She resumed her henna rinses and bought new, flattering clothes, albeit more mature and, so she thought, tasteful than before. She walked the Eureka Wharf at least twice daily, and easily began conversations with people, particularly the fishermen, on the pier.

Fortunately Ralph and Anne's divorce proceedings were fast and neat, allowing them to eagerly proceed with their respective new lives. Ralph was pleasantly surprised, even impressed, that Anne requested no alimony. Just a fair split of their joint assets would do, she insisted. Most pertinent for Anne was that not having a bottomless nest egg would compel her to write and get more books published. It was also pertinent that her significant royalties and speaking fees were all hers, not to be shared with Ralph, and every check she received in the mail from her publishers boosted her new sense of self.

Anne wasn't a bitter, angry divorcee; she wasn't anti-Ralph, anti-husband, or anti-men, she was just learning to enjoy herself for the first time since college. Her new life as a successful author made every day full, as she went to work on her next book, *Confessions of La Sangre*, loaded with verbatim interviews from all the former residents of La Sangre, who were each paid $5,000, covered by her publisher, and not held against her advance, which was $75,000.

In Anne's renewed mind, her marriage to Ralph and raising their two rather strange children were just an intermission in her life; an intermission that had begun when she got pregnant and dropped out of college. She was now going back to the young woman she was sure Ralph had fallen in love with, way back whenever. The intermission now over, she resumed her old life with a vengeance: re-enrolling at University of California at San Francisco as a Sociology major, and taking an apartment in the Haight-Ashbury, which had evolved from a Hippie Haven in the sixties to a New Wave Neighborhood by the 1980s. She let her hair go gray and wore it short. She bought loose, comfortable clothes, made friends, smoked pot, and became the person, the woman, she knew she always was.

Anne occasionally ran into Julie Johnson on the small UCSF campus, and she would enthusiastically invite Julie to her various speaking engagements in the coffee shops of the Haight-Ashbury.

"After all, we're both divorcees now!" Anne smiled broadly as cause for celebration.

"I'm sorry Anne, I can't. All I'm doing is studying and trying to grab some sleep whenever I can," responded the future Dr. Julie Johnson, Pediatrician.

Ralph moved back to his office and a new apartment in Redding where, in addition to his private practice, he resumed his former post as psychiatrist for the five Federal prisons in the Redding area. But this time he did so with a new gusto, a complete about-face from his former lethargy in doing the same, low-paid work. He began having regular discussions with prison clergy, sharing information and insights about the mental health of the prisoners and any religious leanings they may have. Are the prisoners locked in the Human Mobius of hating a God they're convinced doesn't exist? If so, how can that be unlocked? Ralph mentally reviewed his 30+ year caseload. Of those patients that finally broke through, was prayer a part of it, or even necessary? Are there not both insane believers and sane non-believers? Wasn't Ralph once the latter?

Given Ralph's refreshing candor, the clergy with whom he discussed such avant-garde ideas pestered him to write a book—not about the sensational La Sangre crap, of course. There was indeed a large seed bouncing about inside Ralph's always active cranium. Yes, there was some kind of book in there, ready to sprout.

Socially, Ralph's medical colleagues teased him about being a divorced man who's still good looking and in good shape ("Hey Ralph, I go to a great gym, personal trainers, steam room. They'll have you looking like we're back at Redding High School! Remember those cheerleaders when we played football?"). Indeed, as a now-famous psychiatrist Ralph could have any pretty, middle-aged, the-kids-are-long-gone woman he wanted. But Ralph blew them all off; it was the last thing on his mind in his new life, which of course nobody could understand.

All Ralph was certain of was that the middle-aged syndrome—if indeed he ever actually had it—had long passed him by, and by this time in his life he didn't care about sex and he didn't care that he didn't care. He wouldn't even take a lunch date with a single woman, at least not alone, and after a while all the women stopped asking him out. Some thought he might be gay, and his colleagues good-naturedly teased him about that too.

Actually, a low testosterone level was Ralph's self diagnosis, and he was fine with that. The AMA was currently testing testosterone boosters for men, and the medical rumor mill was that the FDA would probably approve it within the next year or two. Maybe he'll reconsider such things then, but in the meantime life was good. If it ain't broke, don't fix it.

Ralph found a church in Redding that he liked, and spent at least one weekend a month in Bakersfield, staying with Doyle and Theresa and the baby. On the drives up and down the California 99 the seed for his book germinated, with a working title of *God and Psychiatry* or *Psychiatry and God*. He'd decide which one later, once the writing commenced.

Maria Malana was found guilty of Murder in the Second Degree, and sentenced to twenty years with possible parole as early as seven years, including time already served in Sacramento, just as her lawyer had promised her. She was transferred to the California Institute of Women in Tehachapi, California. Once the inmates and guards became familiar with her fearless nature and got past the celebrity bit, Maria agreed to facilitate a daily, hour-long meeting of prisoners who were raped and abused by fathers, brothers, men. She opened each meeting with "Well ladies, ready to do a little ball-busting today? You know, if I do this with you I may get out of here in six years, at least that's what my lawyer tells me. So let's all talk, shall we? Who wants to go first? Whose dick do we cut off today?"

"I'll go first!" one of the inmates eagerly raised her hand.

"Matthew?" Lillian found him smoking on the porch of their half-empty La Sangre home. "Telephone. A man named Dean."

"Dean Cunningham?" He stubbed out his cigarette.

"I don't know. He said he knew you from the West Coast Shows." She followed him back inside, and when he didn't go in to use his den phone, she felt free to listen in.

"Hi, Dean?"

"Hey Matt! Well, you sound really married!"

"I am," he looked at Lillian, "very married."

"Never thought I'd see that happen."

"Neither did I," he kept his eyes on his Lillian. "So what's up?"

"Well, the WCS boss-man told me that a new kiddie park is being planned by the Bakersfield Recreation and Park District."

"A new kiddie park in Bakersfield?" Matthew repeated it for Lillian's sake. "You going in on it?"

"Naw. I don't want to live in Bakersfield. But I thought you might be interested."

Matthew didn't respond, but looked at Lillian. They only had a couple weeks left to move out of La Sangre, and they still weren't sure what they were going to do. Now a family of three, with Henry, they had to decide carefully on the living situation.

"Matt, it can't miss! If you can get out of your contact with Codding Town, you can take your Miler coaster down to Bakersfield. And hey, remember Roeding Park?"

"In Fresno?"

"Yeah. They're upgrading some of their kiddie rides. Are you interested in buying the old ones?"

"Which rides?"

"The Ferris Wheel, helicopter ride, whale ride, and they're getting a bigger carousel, going from two-horse abreast to a three, so that's going too."

Matthew whistled. "When's the auction? I'll be there...though I don't know what I'll do with two or three more rides. Codding Kids Town can't take any more rides, according to their contract with the city." He motioned to Lillian to go in and pick up the den extension. "Are those old kiddie rides in good shape?"

"Well, you'll have to check that out for yourself, pal. But Matt, the City of Bakersfield is also looking for someone with experience in carnival rides to be the park's General Manager!"

Lillian accidentally gasped on the extension.

"Was that the little lady I heard?"

"Yes," Lillian answered. "I'm Lillian. Pleased to meet you, Dean."

"Likewise, Lillian. It sounds like this could be a fresh start for the two of you."

"Well..." she took the den phone to the doorway so Matthew could see her. She raised her eyebrows at him and shrugged.

"I don't know, Dean...I'd be working regular hours...."

Lillian's raised eyebrows turned into rolled eyes.

"You already do that at Codding Kids Town, right? But Matt, just think, with your GM pay *and* owning at least a couple of the rides...of course you'd have to incorporate to keep the rides separate from your salary..."

"I know that," Matthew said testily, but it

wasn't toward Dean, it all just seemed so fast... and so right....

"Dean," Lillian took the reins, "do you mind if Matthew and I talk about it and call you back?"

"I got one better, Lillian. How about we all see each other, today. I'm in Santa Rosa, haven't had dinner yet, why don't you two come..."

"No Dean, why don't you come *here* for dinner? You're the one on the road."

"Well I was hoping you'd ask me that. Why else did you think I called you, certainly not to see Matt, that no good carny."

"Matthew?" Lillian asked him after they hung up. "The only doubt in my mind is, do you think we could afford to buy any of those rides? Just the used helicopter ride could go for as much as..." she should have known. Matthew was always talking about the prices of new and used rides.

"$20,000," Matthew said.

"Well...." He had his own modest savings, but the bulk of their estate was from Lillian's mortgage-free La Sangre home, for which Caltrans paid $375,000. "I can't buy all of them myself Lilly, certainly not the carousel. But like Dean says, if I'm getting a GM salary with the city, *plus* owning most of the rides, if not all of them..."

"Matthew," Lillian said in wonder, "this is so perfect! I just know you'll get the General Manager job. You have a good reputation in the industry, don't you? They all know and respect you." She teared up.

"Hey," Matthew came near her, "you know, my strong Nurse Lillian has been doing a lot of crying lately." He pulled her closed. "You're not going all Silly-Lilly on me now, are you?"

She nodded and laughed, head on his shoulder. "Maybe I am, but listen to what we can do. I can get a job at any hospital ER in Bakersfield. We'll get a three...no, a four-bedroom home, a split plan. You and I will have the master suite, and Henry can have two of the bedrooms, one for his movie theater. The fourth bedroom will be..."

"You want your sewing room back?"

"No, it'll be your combo den and guest room with a convertible sofa."

"You'll do all that?" Matthew joined her in tearing up. They hadn't yet discussed exactly what to do with his brother.

"Henry is my family, Matthew, he's my brother-in-law, and I love him. And remember, we talked about him getting a job at a Blockbuster in Santa Rosa, now that he's healed? They must have one in Bakersfield. He did a fine job running The Grand Theater, and the Antique Store here."

"Yeah, sure, we'll find a Blockbuster, or any video rental store that has a bus route from home to the store."

She nodded at him, wet-eyed, excited. "It's all so simple, isn't it?"

"So simple," Matthew repeated, holding his wife. "Lilly, it was so confusing when I went through it, my life, all those years. Now, looking back, during my drive back to Topeka to get Henry, it reads like a finely crafted novel."

On a Monday morning, on the Emerald Ford Employee Bulletin Board, Doyle saw:

CALIFORNIA FORD
DEALERSHIP ASSOC
NOTICE:
BAKERSFIELD FORD
NEEDS LINE MGR.
EFI DIPLOMA REQUIRED
Call for appointment

"Terri," Doyle asked her when he got home. He noticed the packed boxes of books and records on the living room floor, ready for moving. "Oh hon, you should have waited for me to do that." He kissed Theresa and five-month-old Tabitha Athena Seeno in the playpen.

"No, I'm fine." She was at her happiest, stirring soup for dinner, barefoot and yes, pregnant again.

"What do you think about Bakersfield?" he asked her.

"Fun! Sun! Stay! Play!" she answered brightly.

"So," he chuckled and opened the refrigerator for a bottle of Lone Star, "you remember that big old sign on the 99?"

"Doesn't everybody? Did you know it was taken down a couple years ago? The city thought it was 'truck-stop tacky,' and too pathetic a plea for people to move there. But what else can Bakersfield sell, besides the sun?"

"Clean air, affordable housing, beautiful views, near the mountains." Doyle stopped and considered. "But so far away from your family."

"Doyle, you, I and Tabitha..."

"And..." he patted her obvious stomach.

"You name him."

Doyle shrugged, he wasn't sure yet. Maybe Sal, maybe Ralph, he wasn't sure. He told her about the job posting at work.

"Hey!" She looked at him wide-eyed. "Go for it!"

Doyle frowned. "I've only been a mechanic for Emerald Ford for six months. They're not going to give me a promotion so quickly."

"You aced the EFI test, didn't you?"

"Yeah, but..."

"You've never missed a day of work, have you?"

"No."

"You're never late?"

"No."

"You work overtime whenever asked?"

"Yes."

"All your work goes out clean, no returns, right?"

"Right." He sat down at the kitchen table with his beer, shoving some stuff-to-be-packed out of the way.

"And your uniform's always clean, *I* know that. Plus, going from Santa Rosa to Bakersfield is a step down...no, two steps down on the desirability scale. You'll be doing someone else a favor, someone who's dying to get out of Bakersfield like everyone else, someone who'd kill for your job at Emerald Ford in Santa Rosa. It's a rather uneven swap, but who cares? Besides," she raised her eyebrows playfully, "I happen to know you'll get the job."

Doyle gave her a surprised look. "Hey, is that..." he wiggled his hand in the air. "I thought it was...gone."

"So did I." She stopped stirring and went over and sat on his lap, arms around him. "It's kind of sad in a way, but maybe this is my swan song as Madame Athena." She hesitated, then shrugged and kissed him. "But Doyle, gift or not, Bakersfield feels right. Connie is there, living with Grace, and Corey's taking a desk job in the dispatch office at Lawrence Freeman Produce. They're your family, Doyle, and so they're my family. Tabitha and I go where my husband goes, where her father goes."

Doyle couldn't stop looking at her, like when they first met. "Thank you," he told her. "But are you sure you just want to be a wife and mother, in Bakersfield no less?"

"I've already thought about that. If I get bored we can dip into our savings—we'll make a bundle off my Madame Athena house, plus this one—and maybe open up a Greek Bakery. Mama gave me my Yaya's baklava and spanakopita recipes as a wedding present. And I know how to make the phyllo like Yaya did and Mama still does, stretching it paper-thin. It can be a front-picture-window attraction, like you Italians do in your pizza restaurants, spinning the pizzas in the window to bring people in. I'll use my work name: 'Athena's Greek Bakery.' Open only from 6 AM to ten, closed on Sunday for church. I'll serve the best baklava and spanakopita in Bakersfield."

"Are you sure you could do all that?"

"I work hard, like you do. It's in my family." Theresa smiled at him. "It's what we do."

"So okay. But if you're using your Madame Athena name, why don't you put little fortunes in the baklava?"

Theresa looked at him. "Hey, that's not a bad idea."

"Oh sure, like you'd really do that."

"I would!"

"So, what else besides baklava and spanakopita?"

"Well there's Kourabiedes and all the other Greek sugar cookies. And of course we'll have to offer all those horrible American donuts for the great unwashed of Bakersfield. But certainly we'll only serve our robust Greek coffee. Milk, orange juice. That's all we'd need. How does that sound?"

Doyle's transfixed gaze turned into a smile. "You told me that your antennae no longer works. It sounds like it'll happen."

"You know, I'm glad my gift is gone for good. It'll be surprising to see whether or not we really do open a bakery. I like not knowing. It's an adventure. Then again," she shrugged, "who knows, I might *not* do it and just turn into June Cleaver, pearls and all." She gave him a kiss and got up. "The soup is ready. Lamb chops okay?"

Doyle nodded. "Lots of garlic."

"Fun, sun, stay, play!" Theresa sang as she pulled the chops from the fridge and dropped them on the cutting board.

Doyle watched her. Being with her, touching her, just thinking about her, was proof enough that God not only existed, but that He loved Doyle, He loved Theresa, He loved Tabitha. He loved their unborn son.

Matthew looked at the lamb chops. "Hey, do we have a little while?"

Theresa turned the soup down to simmer. "We'll let the chops get room temperature.

They're best that way. Look, Tabitha's asleep."

Grace Freeman was thrilled to have Connie, Corey, and Freeman fill up the empty bedrooms in her Bakersfield home. It was, the Satoris insisted, just until they got their bearings, but between Grace teaching Freeman how to swim in the pool and Connie taking private tennis lessons on Grace's court, and with the approval of all four of Grace's daughters, it was eventually understood that for Connie and Freeman, their living at Grace's home was for the long run.

Corey, of course, had his own young life to live. As far as taking the job in the dispatch department of LFP, he decided to stick with driving. He enjoyed it too much, especially the freedom, and being on the phone and pushing paper forty hours a week could seriously soften and fatten a strong, fit, energetic young man. Grandma Grace certainly understood, while advising Corey that such a deskbound job was always available for him if he got tired of driving. She knew not to bring up college again, it may or may not happen. Corey was a hard worker, with money in the bank, he may not even need college.

"I'm sorry Mr. Freeman," the waiting room warden told Corey indifferently, "Miss Malana does not wish to see you."

It was the second time Corey had tried to

visit Maria, but the rejection didn't matter. His decision to continue driving was made less because he didn't want to sit at a desk, but because he knew that Maria had been transferred to the Tehachapi Women's Prison, just 40 miles east of Bakersfield on the California 58, the main route out of Bakersfield for all points east. After departing Lawrence Freeman Produce with an eastbound load, Corey would easily make a quick stop at Tehachapi, go in and ask to see Maria, and even if she refused to see him, he'd keep on doing it, every time he drove Highway 58, east or west, through the southern range of the Sierra Nevada. Just knowing that *she* knew he had come to see her, and would continue to do so, was all he needed to be happy.

Corey used a small part of his hefty inheritance from Dad Pete to purchase a modest home on two acres in the Sierra Nevada foothills on the California 58, midway between Bakersfield and Tehachapi. It gave him room to park his rig and a great view of the valley. Connie passed the time helping Corey furnish his home, buying utensils and equipment for his kitchen, where she tirelessly cooked casseroles and filled his freezer with individual microwavable containers, for home and the road. Though Connie and Freeman would continue to live with Grace, Corey insisted on a room for each of them in his home, as they often stayed overnight. Corey adopted a four-year-old black Labrador from the Bakersfield SPCA, renamed him 'Niner," and took him on the road for company.

They were all just everyday, working people, living their lives. And they were always there for each other, just a phone call away, or just a short drive up or down California State Route 99 through the ever fertile Central Valley.

SUNDAY, JUNE 14, 1987
FATHER'S DAY

TWENTY

Corey, Connie, Matthew, Lillian, Ralph, Doyle, and Julie met at The Tides Motel at 6 PM as planned. Matthew didn't want to go, because Theresa had just delivered their baby boy, Salvatore Corey Seeno, and he didn't want to leave his son. "No Doyle, you go!" Theresa insisted. "Mama and Papa are here, you need to do this, it's only overnight, so go!"

Henry was regularly scheduled for the busy Saturdays at Bakersfield Video, the store that boasted, true or not, the largest collection of videotapes in the Central Valley. Management loved Henry's customer service; if a customer didn't know the name of a particular movie, they could describe a particular scene and Henry would name the movie ("In Beta or VHS?") and walk them right to it on the racks. Henry hated missing work, especially Saturdays, and besides, he didn't really care to see La Sangre again.

After the greetings and getting set up in their four motel rooms—reserved months in advance with Doyle sharing one with Ralph—they went over to the restaurant to their reserved table for dinner. Hazel and Phil joined them, and they all laughed and brought each other up to date. The motel was never vacant and the Stevens were making tons of money. They promised to come visit them all but...who goes to Bakersfield? They all laughed and agreed that you *drive through* Bakersfield, you don't *go* there, like they did.

"You don't mind if we don't join you tomorrow?" Hazel asked them. "Phil and I have to get this place going. It's a big day. Father's Day is tomorrow and 'The Birds' is going to be on TV tonight. A double whammy."

At five the next morning they boarded the new Ford Econoline Van that Doyle had borrowed from Bakersfield Ford, and drove north to the new La Sangre Vista Point. As Highway One neared the former site of La Sangre, it now wove inland about a quarter mile from the ocean, avoiding the treacherous and infamous hairpin turn south of the town, and moving smoothly through the hills and rejoining the original road a mile north, where Jenner and the windy road to Santa Rosa was. From the northern and southern directions of the One, a turnoff sign read "La Sangre Vista Point. Full Facilities."

Luckily no one was parked there yet; it was still dark, no fog, the stars were fading. Doyle got out of the van and looked around. He hadn't been here since he and Theresa moved out December 31, the final evacuation day; they'd wanted to celebrate one Christmas as a new family in La Sangre.

Doyle perused the parking spaces, the modern restrooms and vending machines, and the secured viewing area at the cliff for tourists and photographers. No one would have known that an actual town was once here, but for a stone and steel monument that commemorated the town as a spill-off village for Bodega Bay fishermen.

Corey approached Doyle, knowing what he was thinking. "I was last here to get the cross from the church, when they started the demolition," he told Doyle. "They weren't just bulldozing the buildings and removing the block foundations, they were digging up the septic tanks, removing the electrical and phone wires. Those bulldozers sculpted a whole new place here, new dirt was brought in from the hills, and they too were sculpted back into shape, nobody would know." He pointed in the general direction of where the La Sangre businesses were. "You can't even tell there were once five businesses here, you can't find any asphalt of the Old Highway One. Not a trace."

"It's like we never existed," Doyle declared softly.

They unloaded the old wooden cross that Corey had salvaged from the La Sangre Christian

Church. He had taken it back to Bakersfield, unbolted the two 4x6's, sanded them, gave them three coats of white, outdoor latex/enamel, rejoined them with new bolts, and the cross was ready for the next Father's Day, today, in 1987.

Somehow Caltrans hadn't touched the well-worn, narrow, sturdy path that extended from behind where the church was up to the top of the 50-foot high rock on the north side of La Sangre, which had presided and protected the small town in its eighty year existence. Along with La Sangre parents' admonishments of "Don't get too close to the cliff" were "Don't fall off the rock!" No child ever did.

Led by Corey and guided by spotlights, they walked single file up the path, taking their turns carrying the cross, a bag of cement, a five gallon bottle of water, two four-foot lengths of rebar, and a shovel. Doyle wore his tool belt.

At the top, Corey showed them all the six-inch wide crack on the top of the rock he had discovered as a child and never forgot. He shoved the cross down into the crack, while Ralph and Doyle mixed and poured the cement into the spaces, fortified by the rebar. They all grabbed hold of the cross and steadied it, Matthew's eye on the level, whiled Corey recalled how his Father Sal, upon his, Connie's and Corey's arrival in La Sangre, had asked the California Coastal Commission if he could place a cross up here, marking the town, but of course the CCC denied his request.

Corey prayed, loudly and proudly, "Jesus, this particular cross, Your cross, is dedicated to my three Fathers: Our Father Who Art In Heaven, and to Salvatore Satori and Peter Freeman."

"Amen!" they all agreed, as the sun brightened the horizon.

Connie openly and joyfully wept, finally and at long last, grateful for the love she had experienced and shared with those two great men. It may have been brief, but time and love are beyond measure. All Connie knew was that it was time to get on with her life.

After the concrete was set, Corey put the the empty bag of concrete into the bucket and carefully led them down to the van.

The La Sangre Vista Point was filling up with cars and people, who were waiting for something, anything, that was left of La Sangre, to happen. They looked up at the cross on top of the rock and the seven people walking carefully down the path, carrying implements.

"They must have just put that cross there," a woman declared.

"I wonder if they're expecting something, something evil. And that's why they put the cross there."

"Do you think anything will happen today?"

"I don't know. Do you think there might be more bodies at the bottom of the cliff?"

"I don't know, we can't see from here. But there's a boat out there, watching us with binoculars. See?"

"Looks like a police boat. Maybe there *is* a body down there!"

"You think?"

"I don't know."

"Well shoot, I *hope* there is. We drove all the way from Altamont."

"The Last Of The La Sangres," as Doyle dubbed themselves, had breakfast back at The Tides, then Julie got into her Nissan and drove to Santa Rosa to spend some time with her parents, before returning to San Francisco and her studies. Ralph got in his Cadillac and drove back to Redding, where he'd do his round of the prisons. The others took the van back to Bakersfield, Doyle excited to be reunited with his newborn son.

They never lost touch with each other, not for the rest of their lives.

TWENTY-ONE

MEMO

DATE: June 22, 1987
FROM: Martin Galiendo, State Attorney General's Office, Sacramento
TO: Sheriff Frank Daley, Sonoma County Sheriff Dept, Santa Rosa

Sheriff Daley,

This is regarding the white wooden cross that someone stuck on top of the rock at the La Sangre Vista Point.

Per Caltrans, the CCC, and the Governor's Office, just let it be. It's wood, probably not treated, and the elements and vandals will take care of it soon enough.

Hey let's have lunch the next time you're in Sac.

Marty Galiendo

Every Father's Day throughout his twenties, Corey Satori Freeman took a gallon of white latex/enamel and drove to the La Sangre Vista Point where, in front of anyone who cared to watch, he walked up the trail to the top of the rock and slapped fresh white paint on the cross.

The old rugged cross is still standing at La Sangre Vista Point on California Highway One.

CPSIA information can be obtained
at www.ICGtesting.com
Printed in the USA
BVHW011015290722
643350BV00009B/55/J